ACTIVATORS

RIDING

Sarah Gaydon

Illustrated by Ken O'Brien and Karen Donnelly

Consultant: Sharon Dodson BHSII

h

*Hodder
Children's
Books*

a division of Hodder Headline plc

Text copyright 1998 © Sarah Gaydon
Illustrations copyright 1998 © Ken O'Brien and Karen Donnelly
Published by Hodder Children's Books 1998

Design by Fiona Webb

The right of Sarah Gaydon and Ken O'Brien and Karen Donnelly to be
identified as the author and illustrators of the work has been asserted by
them in accordance with the Copyright, Designs and Patents Act 1988.

10 9 8 7 6 5 4 3 2 1

A catalogue record for this book is available from the British Library.

ISBN: 0 340 71517 0

The information in this book has been thoroughly researched and
checked for accuracy, and safety advice is given where appropriate.
Neither the author nor the publishers can accept any responsibility for
any loss, injury or damage incurred as a result of using this book.

Hodder Children's Books
a division of Hodder Headline plc
338 Euston Road
London NW1 3BH

Meet the author

In just half an hour, the course of Sarah Gaydon's life changed forever. When she was seven years old, she had her first riding lesson while on holiday with her family in Wales.

Within weeks, ballet shoes and piano practice had been swapped for mud, straw and after-school trips to the stables. Her mother and father soon knew a lot more about Solomon, Amber and Twinkle (the fast grey pony) than they really wanted to. This may be why they encouraged her ambition to become an equestrian journalist.

Today, you'll find Sarah sharing her passion for horses with 60,000 readers of Britain's top-selling fortnightly magazine, *Horse and Pony*. As Deputy Editor, she writes on every aspect of riding and pony care and, after work, puts it all into practice on her horse, Badger.

Introduction

Do you know how to make friends with a pony or jump a course of fences? Perhaps you dream of being an Olympic showjumper or simply long to gallop a pony along the beach. Whatever your ambition, this is the book for you. Find out how to choose a riding school, get the most from your lessons and tackle your first jump. There are masses of practical tips, plus info on breeds, tack, pony care and the stars of the horse world. If you're not pony mad already, you soon will be!

Contents

Pony power

BREEDS • HISTORY
• COLOURS • POINTS OF THE HORSE

Horses and humans have been pals for thousands of years. If you could travel back in time you would see, at different periods in history, knights in heavy armour riding into battle, heavy horses pulling ploughs on farms, and thieves holding up carriages from horseback. Today, four wheels are faster than four legs, but horses are still as popular as ever!

Size wise

Horses and ponies are traditionally measured in 'hands'. One hand is four inches, which is roughly the width of a man's palm. Horses and ponies are also measured in metres and centimetres. A horse is more than 14.2 hands high (hh) (1.47m), while a pony is 14.2hh and under.

Horse breeds

There are more than 100 breeds of horse and pony. They range from the tiny Falabella, which is often no bigger than 7hh (71cm), to huge heavy horses of 18hh (1.83 m) and more, like the Shire. Many horses and ponies are not pure-bred but are described by their type, such as cob, riding pony, or hunter. You're sure to find one that suits you!

The Arab horse is the oldest pure breed in the world. It has a distinctive dished face, compact body and a high tail carriage. Unlike other horses, Arabs have only 17 ribs instead of 18.

The Thoroughbred is the fastest breed of horse in the world and is used for racing. Famous speed stars include Australian legend Phar Lap, winner of 37 races in a four-year career – phew!

It's a fact

All horses and ponies are descendants of a primitive animal called Eohippus. *Its name means 'Dawn Horse' and it lived about 50 million years ago. It was the size of a small dog.*

7

Points of the horse

Do you know a pony's withers from its chestnuts, or its ergots from its fetlocks? If not, get set for a guided tour of the equine body. Knowing which bit goes where will help your riding – and impress your instructor, too!

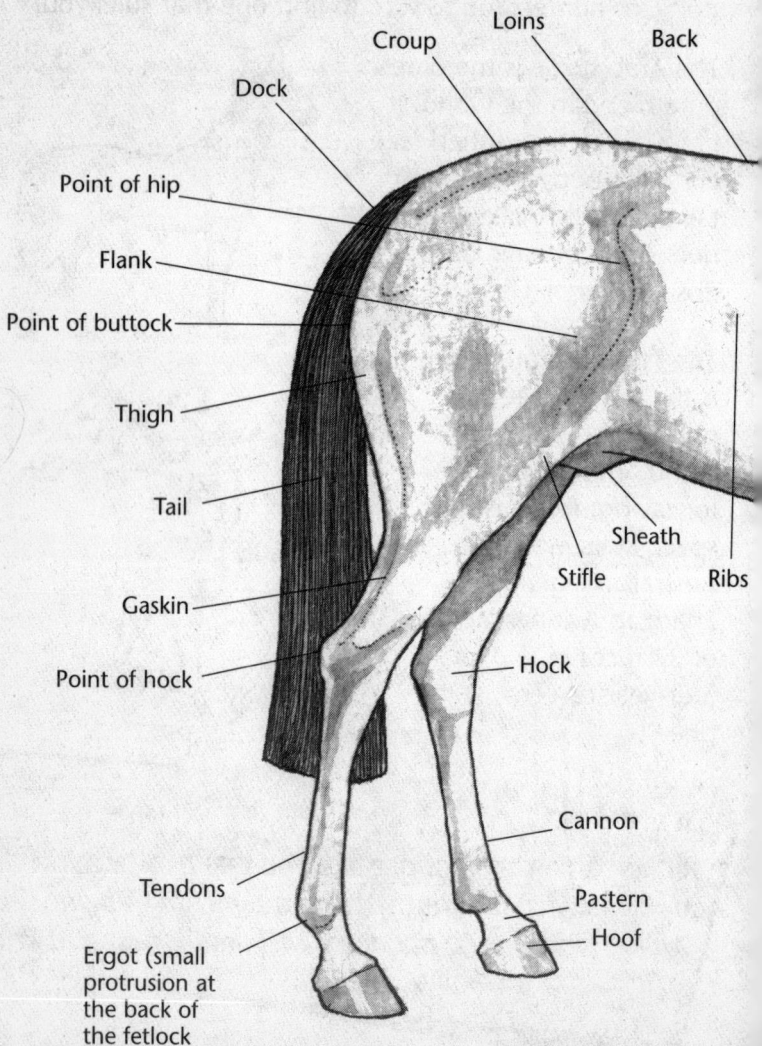

Croup
Loins
Back
Dock
Point of hip
Flank
Point of buttock
Thigh
Tail
Gaskin
Point of hock
Sheath
Stifle
Ribs
Hock
Cannon
Tendons
Pastern
Hoof
Ergot (small protrusion at the back of the fetlock

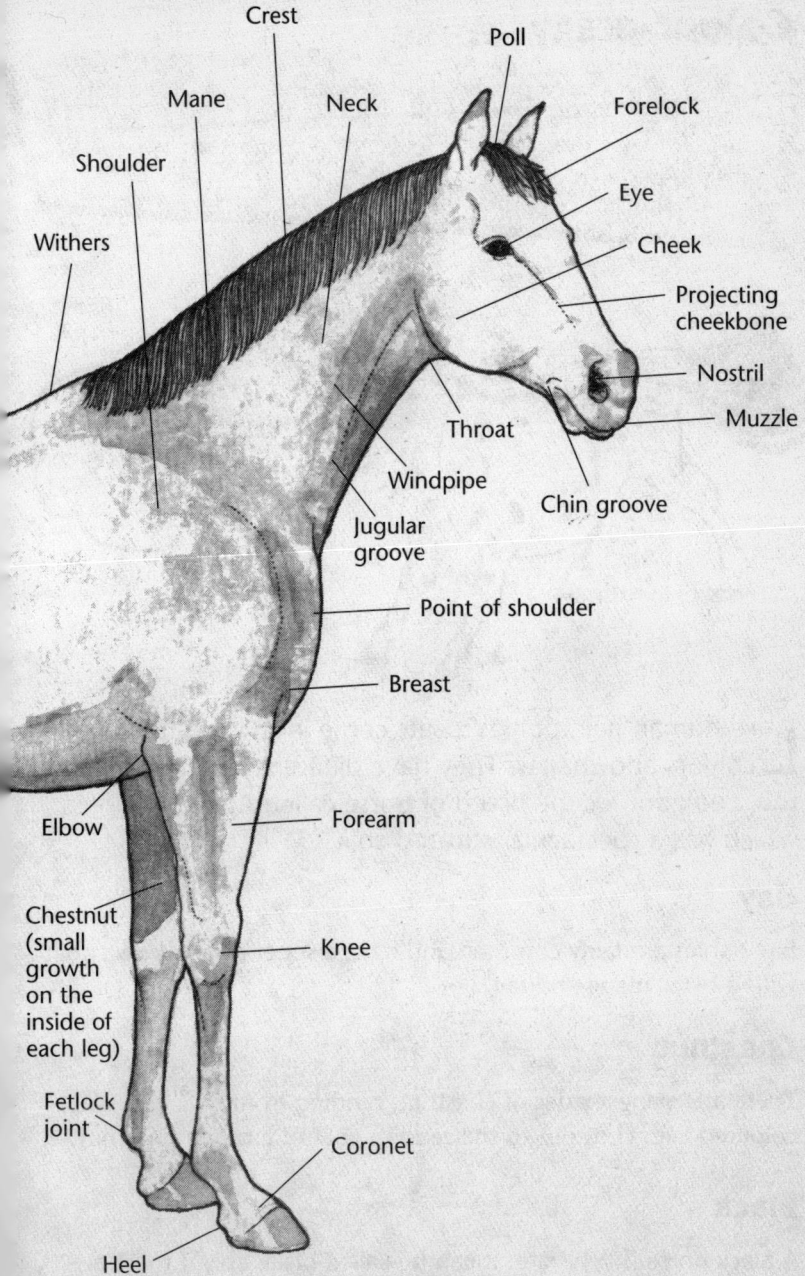

Crest

Poll

Mane

Neck

Forelock

Shoulder

Eye

Cheek

Withers

Projecting
cheekbone

Nostril

Muzzle

Throat

Windpipe

Chin groove

Jugular
groove

Point of shoulder

Breast

Elbow

Forearm

Chestnut
(small
growth
on the
inside of
each leg)

Knee

Fetlock
joint

Coronet

Heel

Colour crazy

Have a competition with your friends and award yourself a point for every one of these pony colours you spot in a day. Whoever scores the most points is the winner.

WHICH COAT SHALL I WEAR TODAY?

Like human hair, ponies' coats come in many different colours and shades. They have different coloured skin too. Look out for the breed of horse called Appaloosa, which has a spectacular spotted coat.

Bay

Bay ponies are fairly common and have a super-smart brown coat with a black mane and tail.

Chestnut

There are many shades of chestnut, ranging from milk-chocolate-coloured liver chestnut to the reddish coat of a bright chestnut.

Black

A black horse is very rare. It can be called black only if there are no brown hairs at all. Otherwise it is called brown.

Grey

Meet the grey family. They all have black skin and their coats are a mixture of white and black hairs. As well as plain grey, they can be iron grey (very dark), dappled grey (light patches on a darker background) and fleabitten grey (specks of grey or brown on a light coat). Greys may be gorgeous, but they can't hide their age – as they get older, their coats turn almost white!

Dappled grey

Iron grey

Fleabitten grey

Piebald/Skewbald

What could be cooler than a coat covered in patches? Black and white ponies are called piebald while ponies with patches of white and any other colour except black are called skewbald.

Dun

Dun ponies can be golden or mouse-coloured with a black skin. They usually have a black mane and tail.

Palomino

Gorgeous palominos are golden coloured with a much paler mane and tail – sometimes almost white.

Roan

Roans can be strawberry (a mixture of white and chestnut hairs), blue (white and black hairs), or red (white and bay hairs).

On your marks!

If you thought socks and stockings were just for humans, think again! Every pony on the planet has markings that can be used to identify it – just like your fingerprints. Many have distinctive white hair on their faces and legs.

Face markings

The most common face markings are a white face, blaze, stripe, star and snip. Some ponies have a combination of these, so don't be surprised if you spot one with a star AND a stripe.

Blaze

White face

Snip

Stripe

Star

Leg markings

With four legs per pony, you'll get to see all sorts of shapes and sizes of pattern. White from the foot up to the knee or hock is usually called a sock. When the white extends higher, often over the knee or hock it is called a stocking. There are lots of markings in between.

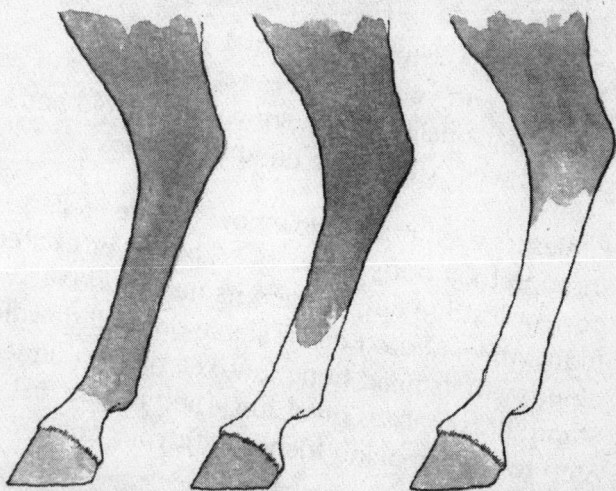

White pastern   White sock   White stocking

FACTFILE

- A prophet's thumbmark is a small indentation on a pony's neck – it's meant to be lucky!
- The pink marks sometimes found around a pony's muzzle are known as flesh marks.
- If a pony is injured, the hair that grows back over the wound is often white.
- A pony can be identified by the swirls of hair on its body, known as whorls. These cannot be disguised – unlike white markings.
- A black stripe along the back is called a dorsal stripe. Duns often have one of these.

Horsey body language

IS YOUR PONY HAPPY, BORED, SAD OR MAD?

Spend time with the ponies at your riding school and you'll discover each one has a unique personality. Some are naturally bold and curious, while others are timid or grumpy.

Ponies let each other know how they're feeling through their body language. A happy or excited pony will stride out, holding its head and tail high, while a bored or miserable one will dawdle along with its head hung low. Learning to understand 'horse talk' is great fun – and it's the first step towards making friends with your pony.

Scent-sational!

This strange face is known as 'flehmen' and a pony makes it when it is closely examining an unusual smell. Ponies have an excellent sense of smell and can identify friends simply by blowing gently into each other's nostrils.

Ear Ear!

Ears are a dead giveaway to a pony's state of mind. Pricked ones say 'I'm alert and ready for action,' but very floppy, downward-turned ones mean the pony is tired or in pain. Most common are ears which face sideways – you'll see them on a relaxed pony that is eating or resting. Stand clear if a pony has its ears pinned flat back against its head and is baring its teeth. This is a sign of anger and a warning to stay away.

A happy pony.

Making friends

Watch a group of ponies in the field and you'll often see friends standing nose to tail, enjoying a spot of mutual grooming. This is something you can try with your favourite pony. Stand next to its shoulder and gently scratch its withers with your hand. If the pony likes you, it may try to return the favour!

Mutual grooming is a handy way of cleaning and scratching those hard-to-reach places.

2 The right start

You've finally persuaded your parents to pay for riding lessons – now all you need to do is find a riding school and a good instructor.

Q How do I find a riding school?

A It's easy! Ask horsey friends or look in the telephone directory for a list of stables in your area. If possible, choose one that is approved by a national riding association. Draw up a shortlist of stables that sound suitable. Telephone each one and arrange a time to go and look around BEFORE you book a lesson.

Q What questions should I ask when I visit a riding school for the first time?

A Find out what facilities are available – such as a manege (outdoor riding arena), an indoor school (useful in bad weather), a cross-country course or showjumps. Ask to be shown around the yard. The ponies should be happy, alert and well cared for and the yard should be clean and tidy. The staff should be helpful and willing to answer all your questions. Watch other riders having a lesson – are they learning a lot and having fun?

A stableyard should look clean and tidy.

Q How much should I expect to pay for a lesson?

A Prices vary depending on the type and length of lesson and the qualifications of the instructor. Lessons may be half, three-quarters or one hour long. A group lesson will cost less than the same-length private lesson on your own. As a rough guide, an hour's group lesson will cost about the same as a new CD. Most beginners start with private lessons and then join a group as they improve.

What to wear

There's no need to spend loads of money on expensive riding gear when you're starting out. The most important thing is that your clothes are practical, comfortable and safe. Ask at the stables what they recommend for you to wear.

Hat

A riding hat that meets current safety standards is essential and in many countries it is illegal not to wear one. Most riding schools have hats that pupils can borrow free of charge but if you do decide to continue riding, it's best to buy your own. Choose between a traditional velvet riding hat or a jockey skull cap with a cover, called a silk.

Boots

Sturdy shoes or boots with a small, flat heel are fine for your first few lessons. Later on, you'll probably want to buy long riding boots (made of leather or rubber) or a pair of short jodhpur boots. Both are specially designed to help you stay comfortable and secure in the saddle. Never wear trainers, high heels or wellingtons because these get stuck in the stirrup irons, which is dangerous if you fall off.

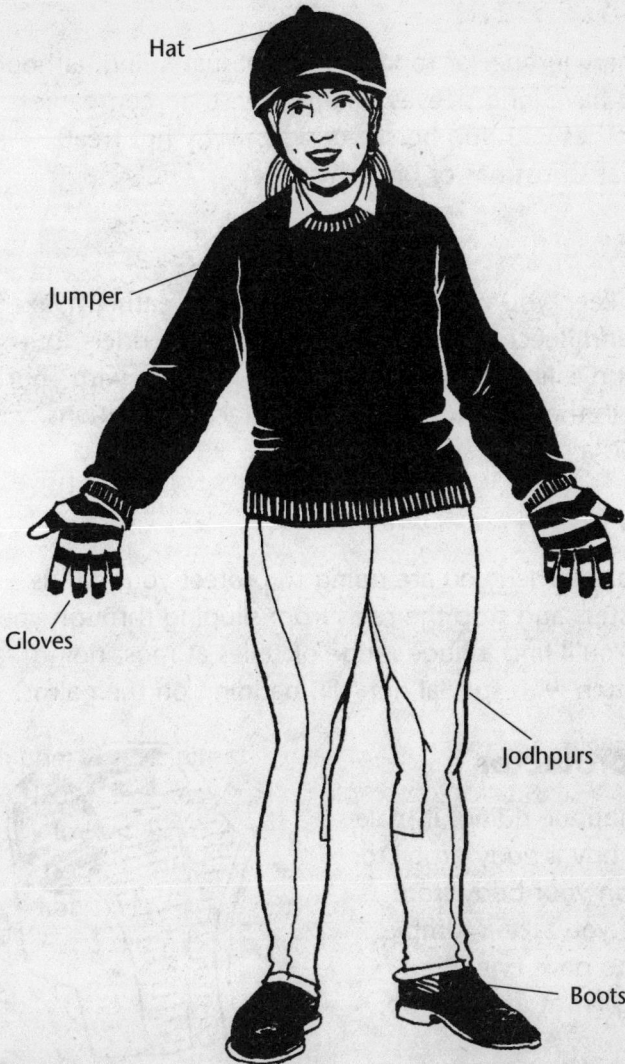

Hat

Jumper

Gloves

Jodhpurs

Boots

Jodhpurs

Thick leggings or jeans are OK for your first lesson, but
you'll soon want to get your legs into a pair of jodhpurs.
These are close-fitting stretchy trousers designed for
maximum comfort in the saddle.

Jumper

An ordinary jumper or top is fine for casual riding, although it should have long sleeves. Many equestrian companies make clothes with fun horsey designs. Why not treat yourself at Christmas or birthday-time?

Jacket

This will keep you warm and snug in cold weather. Waxed, quilted and fleece jackets are all popular with riders, but any design is fine so long as it doesn't interfere with your position in the saddle. Later, if you enter competitions, you may need a smart hacking jacket.

Gloves

Wear gloves when you are riding to protect your hands from blisters and stop the reins from slipping through your fingers. You'll find a huge range of styles at most riding shops, often with special non-slip padding on the palms.

Body protector

If you continue riding, it makes sense to buy a body protector to cushion your body from bumps if you take a tumble. It's best to have one fitted by an expert at a tack shop.

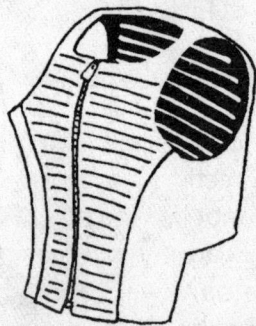

Hair scare!

It helps if you can see where you're going when you're on horseback! If you have long hair, use a hairband or a hairnet to keep it neat, tidy and out of your eyes.

3 | **Your first lessons**

MEETING YOUR PONY
• MOUNTING • DISMOUNTING

Riding a pony for the first time is an exciting experience. Just imagine, it could be the start of a life-long hobby or a fantastic career with horses. Even top riders had to begin with the basics!

Your first lesson will be on an experienced 'schoolmaster' pony that has seen plenty of beginners before you. Don't worry if you make mistakes. A good, qualified instructor will ensure you are safe and have plenty of fun both in and out of the saddle.

Pleased to meet you

Once your instructor has checked you are kitted out correctly, he or she will introduce you to your pony. Ponies cannot see directly in front or behind them because their eyes are set wide apart on the sides of their faces. For this reason, always approach a pony at an angle from the front, otherwise it may get a fright when it suddenly catches sight of you!

Always approach a pony from the front and side.

CO020 29541 CX.

Get to grips with your pony's gear!

The gear that your pony wears when you ride it is called tack. It is designed to help you control your pony. The two items of tack every rider needs to know about are the saddle and bridle.

The saddle

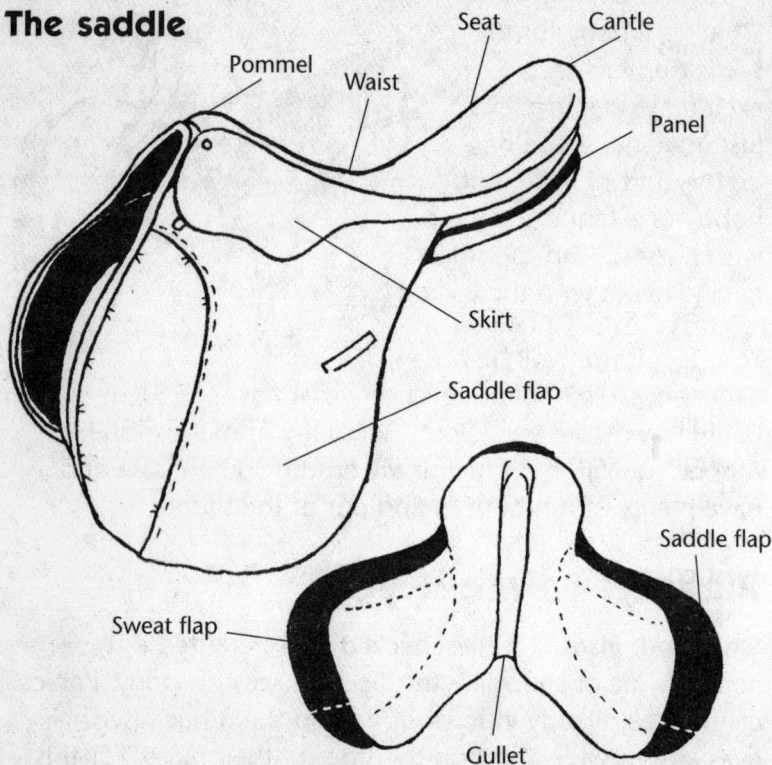

A general-purpose saddle from above and underneath.

A saddle helps a rider feel secure and should be comfortable for both you and the pony. The most popular type of saddle is a general-purpose one. This is suitable for most activities, including hacking and jumping. There are also specialist saddles for sports such as racing, jumping, dressage and showing.

The bridle

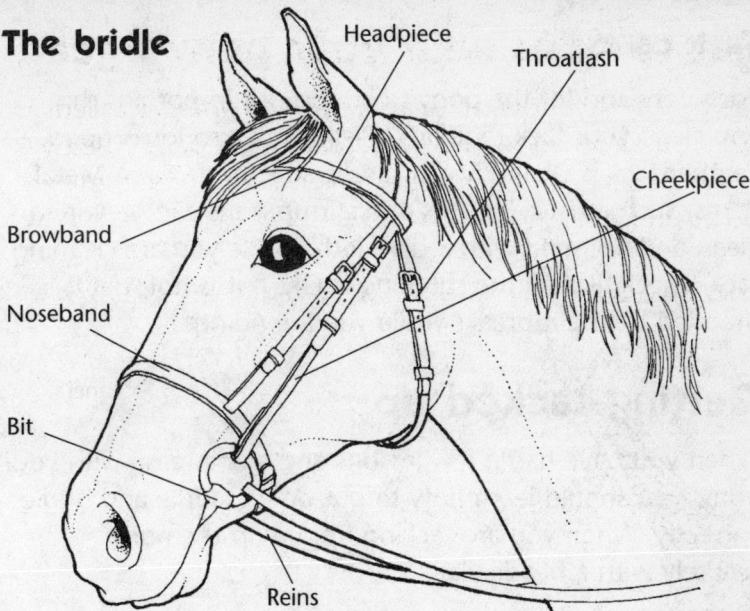

Headpiece
Throatlash
Cheekpiece
Browband
Noseband
Bit
Reins

This pony is wearing a snaffle bridle.

A bridle helps you control a pony's speed and direction through the bit and reins. There are four main types of bridle – the snaffle, double, pelham and bitless. The pony you ride will probably have a snaffle bridle, which is the most common.

Bits

There are many different types of bit, which can be made from stainless steel, rubber or vulcanite. See if you can spot these ones on ponies at your riding school.

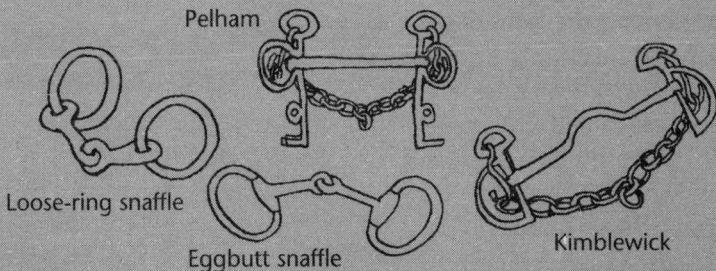

Pelham

Loose-ring snaffle

Eggbutt snaffle

Kimblewick

Tack care

For safety and for the pony's comfort, it's important that you clean your tack regularly. Clean tack also looks good. Leather tack is cleaned with saddle soap and water. Metal items, such as buckles, bits and stirrup irons can be wiped clean and polished with a dry cloth. While you are cleaning tack, check that all the stitching is OK. If it is not, get it mended before it breaks while you are riding.

Getting tacked up

When you have had a few lessons and feel at ease with your pony, you should learn how to put on its saddle and bridle correctly. When you are tacking up, tie up the pony securely with a headcollar.

Putting on a saddle ...

Place the girth across the top of the saddle. Hold the saddle with the pommel in your left hand and the cantle in your right hand. Stand at your pony's nearside and gently place the saddle on the pony, on top of the saddle cloth if there is one, in front of the withers. Slide the saddle and saddle cloth back into place. Walk around the front of the pony and pull the girth down. Walk back to the nearside, reach underneath the pony, pick up the girth and fasten it loosely on the nearside. Tighten the girth when you are ready to get on.

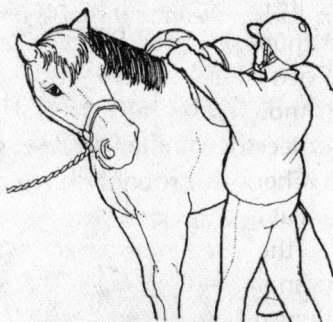

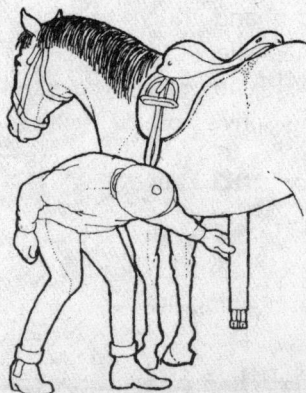

...and taking it off

Run up both stirrup irons and unbuckle the girth from the nearside. Gently lift off the saddle and saddle cloth together and place the girth across the saddle.

Putting on a bridle...

Make sure the noseband and throatlash are undone. Put the reins over the pony's head, then take off the headcollar while you put on the bridle. Hold the bridle in front of the pony's face with your right hand. Guide the bit into the pony's mouth with your left hand. Encourage the pony to open its mouth by slipping your thumb into the gap between its teeth at the side of its mouth. Ease the headpiece over the pony's ears. Check that everything is lying flat and straight, then fasten the throatlash so that you can fit four fingers underneath. Fasten the noseband underneath the cheek pieces so that you can fit two fingers between it and the pony's nose.

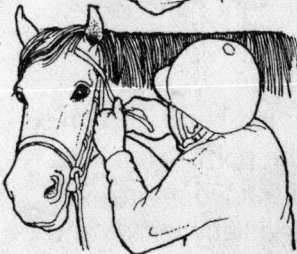

... and taking it off

Undo the noseband and throatlash then slip the head-piece and reins over the pony's head. Don't let the bit bang the pony's teeth.

Top tip

Once you've tacked up, stretch each of your pony's front legs forwards in turn. This will help smooth out any folds of skin trapped underneath the girth.

25

Lead the way

One of your first tasks will be to lead your pony from its stable with the help of your instructor. Take the reins over the pony's head and stand at its left shoulder. This is called its nearside shoulder. (The other one is its offside shoulder.) Hold the reins in your right hand loosely under its chin. Hold the other end of the reins in your left hand. Walk next to the pony's shoulder. A well-trained animal will walk quietly beside you without pulling or dragging behind.

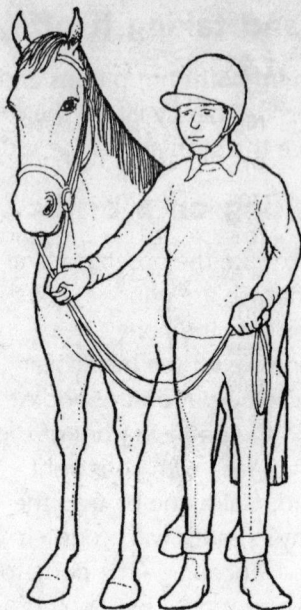

Leading a pony from the nearside.

Turnabout!

With four feet to think about, ponies need plenty of room to turn. When you want to change direction, always turn a pony away from you. Walk in a large circle, with you on the outside of it.

Avoid crushed toes – always turn your pony away from you!

Stay safe

- NEVER wrap the reins around your hand or let them trail on the ground when leading a pony. If the pony panics, you could both become tangled up and badly hurt.
- It is best to wear a riding hat whenever you handle ponies – especially ones you don't know. Try to be confident and firm, even if you don't feel it. Most ponies will be able to sense if you are nervous, and cheeky ones may try to take advantage. You must be in charge.

- Ponies really respond to the tone of your voice, so don't be afraid to speak up! Talk to your pony to reassure it, tell it off – or simply let it know where you are.

Up and over

If you've got flexible legs and a head for heights, you'll have no problems mastering the art of mounting and dismounting. The first few times you try, your instructor will probably hold your pony, so you can concentrate on your technique. Don't worry if you find getting on and off difficult at first. Like most things, it becomes easier with practice.

WHAT IS SHE DOING?

Get set

Before mounting, always make these final checks:
- The reins are over your pony's head.
- The girth is tight enough to prevent the saddle from slipping.
- The stirrup irons are pulled down on both sides.
- The stirrup leathers are the right length. As a rough guide, the base of the stirrup iron should touch your armpit when your finger tips are on the stirrup bar.
- The saddle flaps are lying flat.
- The safety catches on the stirrup bars are down. If you're unlucky enough to fall off and get your foot stuck in the stirrup, this allows the leathers to be released.

How to mount

STEP 1

Stand by your pony's nearside shoulder, facing its tail. Hold the reins in your left hand, keeping them short enough to prevent your pony from wandering off. Place your left hand on your pony's withers.

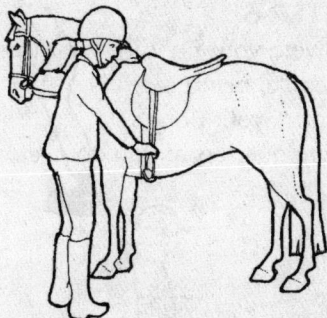

STEP 2

With your right hand, take the stirrup iron and turn it in a clockwise direction to face towards you.

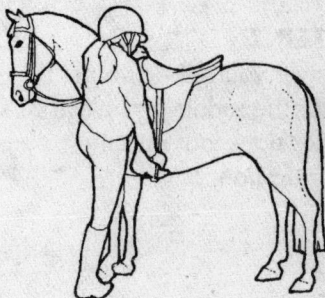

STEP 3

Place your left foot in the stirrup iron. Press down with your toe, so you don't accidentally jab your pony in its side.

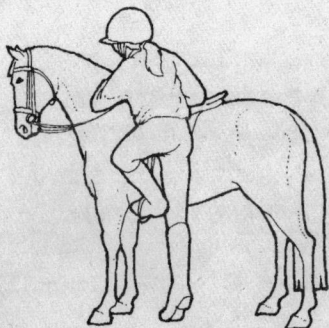

STEP 4

Hop around on your right foot and turn your body so you're facing the saddle. Place your right hand on the waist (middle) of the saddle, to help you keep your balance when you finally spring up.

29

STEP 5

Now for the tricky bit. Transfer your weight to your left foot and lightly spring up, straightening both your knees and moving your right hand forwards as you do so. Do not pull yourself up by the saddle. ▶

STEP 6

◀ Swing your right leg over the saddle, being careful not to knock your pony's hindquarters as you go over.

STEP 7

Lower yourself down gently into the saddle and place your right foot into the stirrup iron. ▶

Be the best

Although it's usual to mount from the nearside of your pony, it's a good idea to practise mounting from the offside, too. This skill will improve your suppleness and agility and save vital seconds in gymkhana games or an emergency, when speed is all-important.

Or try this!

There's more than one way to get into the saddle. Here are some alternative methods you might see people using. Your instructor will teach you how to mount from a mounting block and how to get a leg-up.

Mounting block

A mounting block is a small platform with two or three steps. It is useful if you cannot reach the stirrup iron, or you find it hard to spring into the saddle from the ground. Using a mounting block is easier for the rider and also puts less strain on the pony's back.

Leg-up

This is a quick way of mounting with the help of an assistant and is useful for getting on a big pony or one that won't stand still.

Vaulting

You'll see some riders vault on their ponies at high speed during gymkhana games. Although it looks easy, you need to be very experienced and athletic to manage it. Don't ever attempt to vault on your pony without the help of your instructor!

Dismounting

At the end of a lesson, your instructor will ask you to turn your pony into the centre of the school and halt, ready to dismount. As with mounting, it's usual to do this from the nearside. Here's how:

STEP 1
Remove both feet from the stirrups and place the reins in your left hand. Rest your left hand on your pony's neck and lean forwards.

STEP 2
Place your right hand on the pommel (front) of the saddle. Swing your right leg up and over the saddle behind you, keeping it clear of your pony's hindquarters.

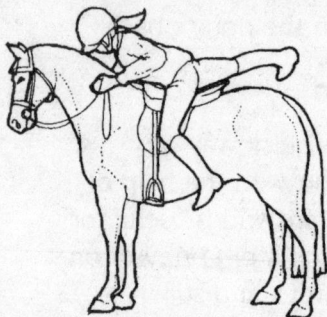

STEP 3
Slip quietly to the ground with your knees bent so you don't jar your legs as you land. Remember to keep hold of the reins in case your pony decides to walk off.

Alternative methods

In some countries, such as Australia, you will be taught to dismount leaving your left foot in the stirrup. Instead of slipping to the ground after you have swung your right leg over, you will step down, then remove your left foot.

Never dismount by swinging your leg over the front of the saddle. You will have to let go of the reins as you jump off so you'll have no control over your pony if it moves away.

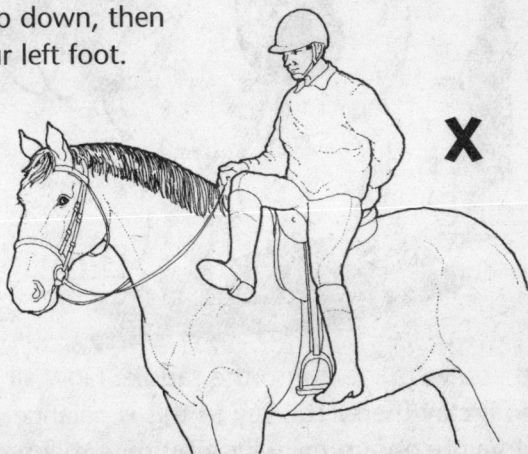

Don't forget!

Before you lead your pony away once you have dismounted, you should:

- Slide both stirrups to the top of the leathers and push the ends back through the stirrups. This is called running up the stirrups.
- Loosen your pony's girth a couple of holes.
- Take the reins over its head.

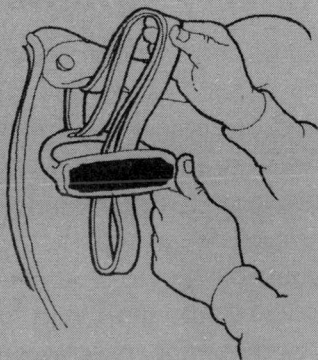

Running up a stirrup.

In the saddle

TACK CHECKS • YOUR POSITION

Relax! You've made it into the saddle. Now all you've got to do is stay there. The key to this is balance. Anyone can feel secure on a pony with a bit of work on their position and a few adjustments to their tack.

Tummy trouble

Some cheeky ponies have a nasty habit of blowing out their tummy when a rider does up the girth so it is too loose when the pony relaxes. So, as soon as you're mounted, you need to check the girth. Aim to fit just three fingers between the girth and your pony.

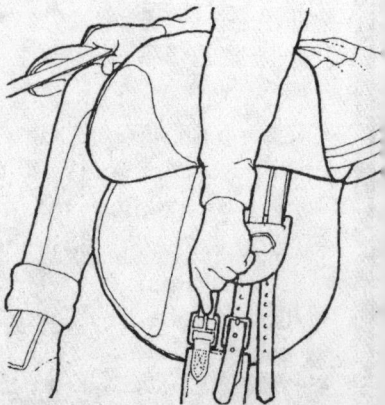

Tightening the girth.

You usually tighten the girth on the nearside. Move your leg in front of the saddle and lift the saddle flap with your right hand. Use your other hand to move the buckle up a few holes on the girth straps. Feel for the hole with your finger. Check the girth again once you've ridden your pony around for a few minutes.

Great lengths

The stirrups should help you feel secure and comfortable when riding, so it's important they're the right length. To check, take your feet out of the stirrups and let them hang loosely against your pony's sides. If your stirrups are the correct length, the bottom of each iron should rest on or just above your ankle bone. If not, you'll need to alter them. Keep your foot in the stirrup and undo the buckle on the stirrup leather. Fasten it a couple of holes higher or lower. For comfort, pull the back of the leather down so the buckle comes up close to the stirrup bar. Tuck the end of the leather into its keeper on the saddle flap.

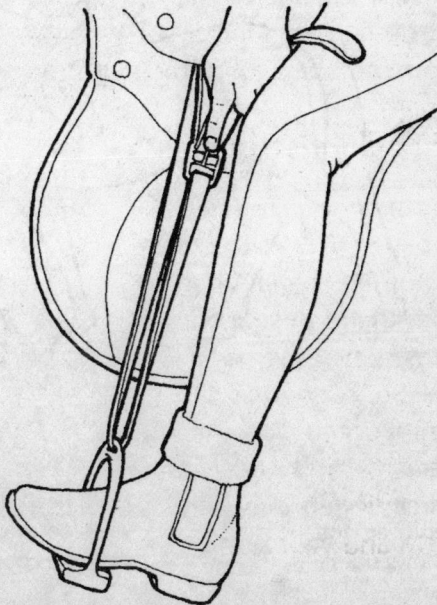

Adjusting the stirrups.

Your position

HEAD: Hold your head high and look where you're going.

BACK AND SHOULDERS: Sit up tall and keep your upper body straight.

ARMS: Keep your arms relaxed and slightly bent, with your elbows close to your sides.

SEAT: Sit in the centre of the saddle, with your weight evenly distributed on both your seatbones.

HANDS: Hold your hands level above the pony's withers, a few centimetres apart and with your thumbs on top.

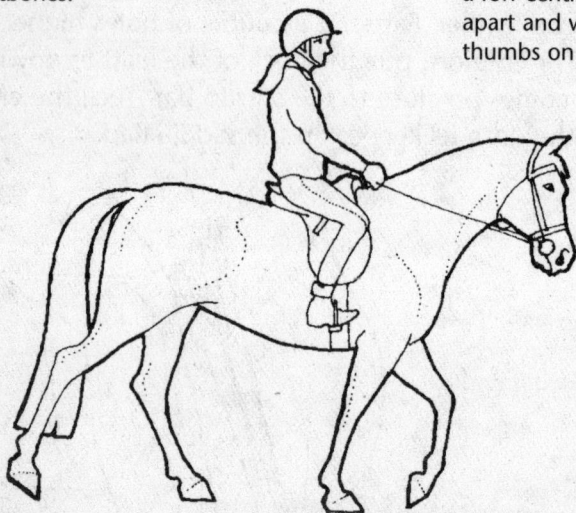

LEGS: Wrap your legs gently around your pony's sides.

FEET: Keep the stirrups on the balls of your feet with your heels down and your toes pointing forwards.

When you are sitting correctly in the saddle, you will be able to control your pony better, and it will understand more easily what you are asking it to do.

Line up!

If you're sitting correctly, a friend should be able to draw an imaginary straight line from your shoulder, through your hip to your heel.

Taking up the reins...

The reins are your way of communicating with your pony, through the bit in its mouth. Use them to control your pony's speed and direction, but be gentle. Never haul on the reins or hang on them for balance because your pony will end up with a very sore mouth – ouch!

Place the reins across the palm of each hand, running them between the thumb and first finger and third and little finger.

Loop the spare rein back over your index finger so it hangs down towards your pony's shoulder. Hold your hands sideways with your thumbs on top, as if your were carrying two cups of tea.

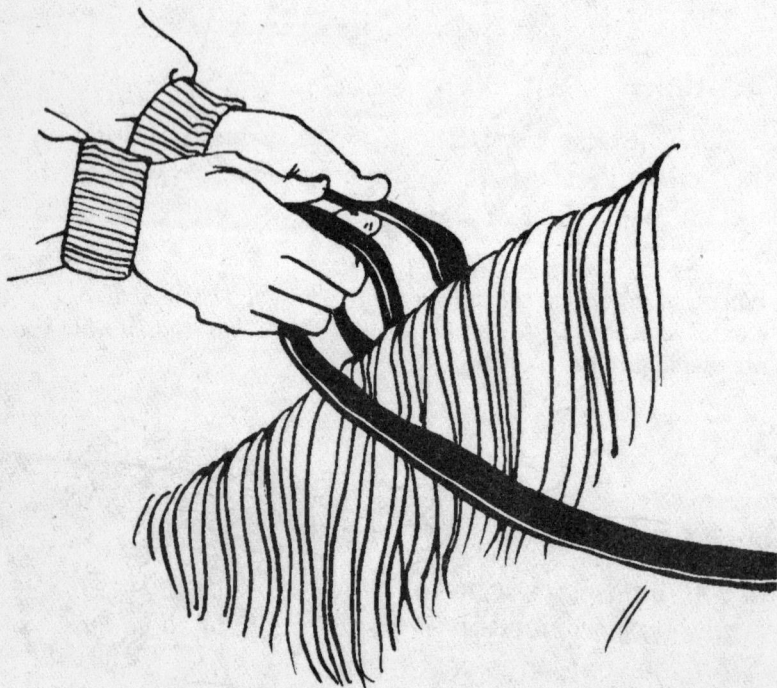

Q My instructor often tells me to 'take up a contact' with my pony's mouth. What does this mean?

A The contact is the link between your hands and your pony's mouth, through the bit and reins. You should aim for a light contact at all times, when you can just feel the pony's mouth.

Q I find it difficult to keep my hands still when I ride. What can I do?

A Relax! It's important to keep your hands as still as possible, but you must also allow them to move backwards and forwards with the movement of your pony's head and neck. Otherwise, your pony won't be able to stride out freely. Think of the reins as pieces of elastic that gently stretch but never go baggy or too tight in your hands.

Tea-time!

If you want to keep your hands in the correct position, think of the two cups of tea you are pretending to carry and don't spill a single drop!

Line up!

Here's a quick and easy way to find out if you're holding your hands in the correct position. Ask a friend to look at your arms and see if they can draw an imaginary straight line from your elbow, along the reins to your pony's mouth. If they can, you've got it right!

Brainbusters

1 What is the marking on this pony's face called?

2 What is the name of the piece of bridle that goes under a pony's throat?

3 Unscramble the following anagram to reveal a breed of pony:

ASNDHLET

4 What sort of mood is your pony likely to be in if its ears are flat back against its head?

5 What type of bit is this?

6 Which breed of horse is famous for its dished face?

7 Where would you find a fetlock?

8 Pick the odd one out: strawberry, yellow, blue

9 What is a manege?

10 Is this grey pony iron, dappled or fleabitten?

• You'll find the answers on page 122!

5 Walk this way

THE AIDS • WALK • HALT • TURNING

So you want some excitement in your life. Then let's get moving! One of the first things you need to learn is how to start, stop and turn your pony, using the correct aids. Aids are the signals you give to tell your pony to change direction or speed, or stop. There are two types of aid you can use to communicate with your pony. These are known as natural and artificial.

Natural aids

The natural aids are your legs, hands, seat and voice.

HANDS: Your hands hold the reins and control your pony's speed and direction.

VOICE: The tone of your voice can encourage, praise or calm your pony.

LEGS: Use your legs to ask your pony to go faster, stay on a straight line or turn.

SEAT: As you become a more experienced rider, you'll be able to use your back and seat muscles to influence your pony's way of going. Used together with your leg aids, you can help your pony stay balanced and ask it to move with more impulsion (energy).

43

Artificial aids

Sometimes, no matter how hard you try, your pony won't respond to your natural aids. This is when an artificial aid, such as a whip, comes in handy. A sharp smack behind your leg will soon wake your pony up and get it listening to you again. Other artificial aids are spurs and a martingale.

Hold your whip in the palm of your inside hand (the one nearest the centre of the school), so it lies flat across your thigh. Unless it's a long schooling whip, you'll need to take your hand off the reins to use it.

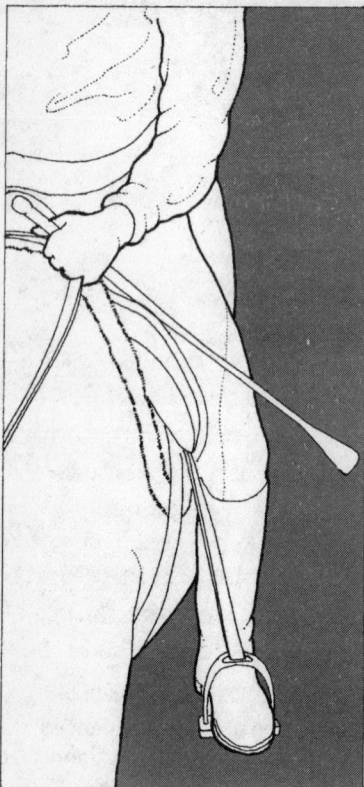

How to hold a whip.

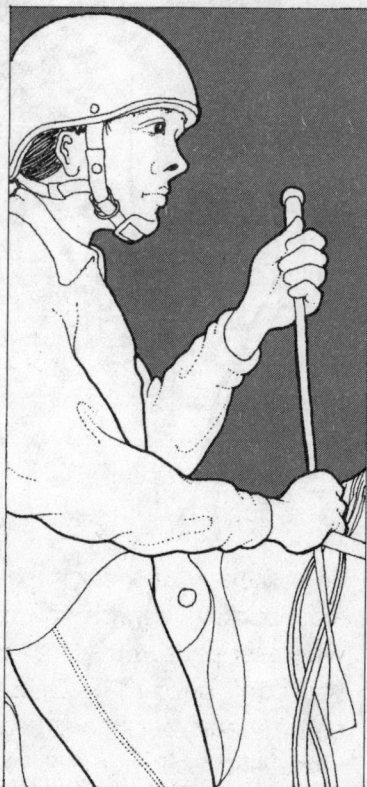

When you change direction, you'll need to swap your whip over to the inside again.

Changing paces

A transition is another name for a change of pace. An upwards transition is when you ask your pony to move up a pace – for example, from walk into trot or trot into canter. A downwards transition is when you switch to a slower pace, such as from trot to walk or from walk to halt.

To make any of these transitions, you must use the correct aids. Luckily, the aids you use to go faster are the same whatever pace you're in – as are the aids to go slower. So you don't need to be Einstein to get moving! Simply co-ordinate your hands, legs and seat and have a quick word with your pony!

Halt... into walk

When making any transition, your aids should be clear, quick and almost invisible to anyone watching you. That's easier said than done if you're on a lazy pony, but it is possible – you won't see top dressage riders flapping their legs madly to get their horses going. If your pony doesn't listen to your aids, repeat them more strongly, or back them up with a tap of your whip.

HALT:

Your pony should be standing square with its weight evenly distributed on all four feet. Prepare for the transition by closing your fingers on the reins and sitting as tall as you can in the saddle.

TRANSITION:

Use your legs to gently squeeze your pony's sides, just behind the girth. Relax the pressure as soon as your pony walks forwards.

WALK:

Once in walk, concentrate on staying relaxed and sitting deep in the saddle. Keep your legs still and your rein contact steady, but allow your hands to follow the movement of your pony's head and neck.

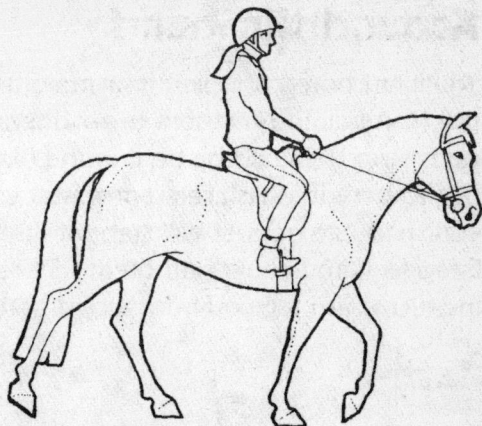

Best foot forward

When you use your legs to give an aid, try to keep your weight in your heels. If you kick upwards with your heels, you'll tip forwards and become unbalanced.

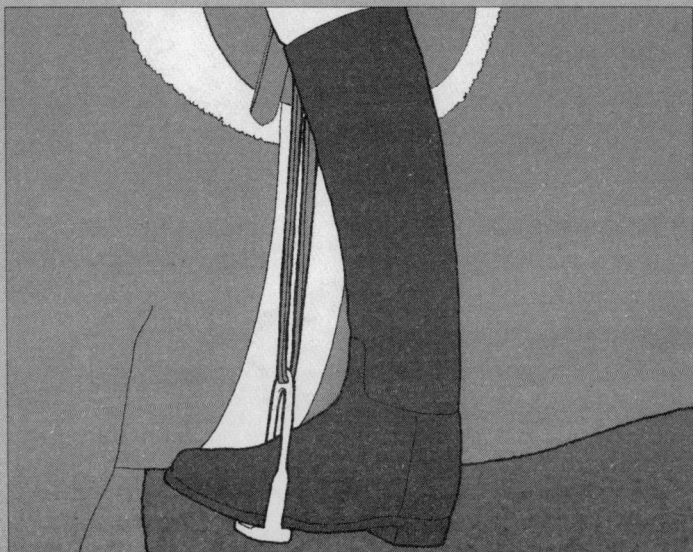

Around the bend

You'll get bored of going in a straight line pretty quickly, so the next skill to practise is turning. When riding a turn, your pony's body should be bent in the direction it's going – but not so bent it looks like a banana! If you're doing it right, your pony's hind feet will step on the imprints left by its front feet. You could hop off and have a look, but your instructor will tell you how you're getting on!

The aids to turn

- Turn your head a little to look where you want to go. This helps warn your pony of a change in direction, because it will sense the shift in your balance.
- Squeeze the inside rein with your hand to guide your pony into the turn.
- Use your outside rein to control your pony's speed and the amount of bend.
- Your inside leg should stay on the girth to keep your pony moving forwards.
- Put your outside leg just behind the girth to stop your pony's quarters from swinging out.

Four tips for top turns!

1 Plan your turn. Aim for a gentle curve rather than a sharp bend.
2 Help your pony stay balanced by sitting tall and straight in the saddle. Don't look down or lean to the inside.
3 Keep a steady rhythm. Your pony doesn't need to slow down or speed up as it turns.
4 Let your outside hand move forwards slightly as your pony turns its head, and keep your hands level.

49

About turn!

Turns are tricky to ride well – sometimes it'll feel as if your pony's front end and hindquarters are doing completely different things. If you get in a mess, straighten up and try again. Have a go at some simple turns across the school to change direction and ride a few 20-metre circles in walk. The more you practise, the quicker you'll be able to adjust your aids to correct any faults.

The correct bend

Quarters sticking out

Quarters sticking in

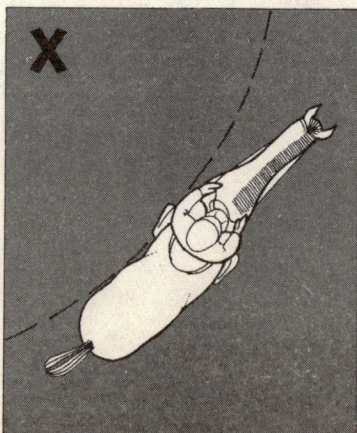

Shoulder too far in.

50

How do I stop?

If all that turning has made you dizzy, it could be time to apply the brakes, slow the pace and bring your pony back to halt.

To do this, sit tall and deep in the saddle and apply gentle pressure with both your legs. At the same time, close your hands to squeeze the reins until your pony gets the message. Relax your aids as soon as you come to a standstill.

Say thanks!

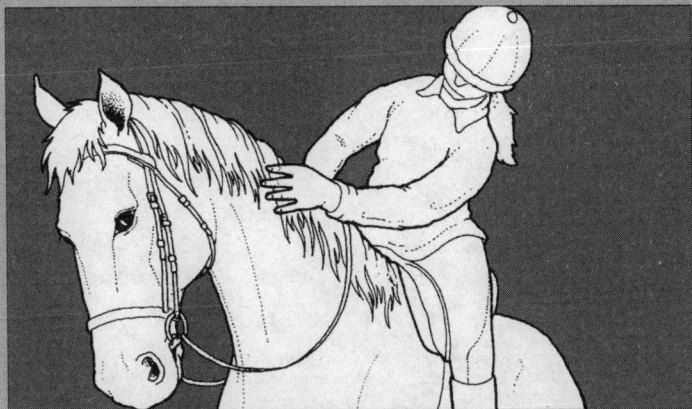

Show your pony you love it!

At the end of your lesson, let your pony walk around on a long rein to cool off and relax its muscles. Give it a pat on the neck to say 'thanks'.

When you have put your pony away in its stable, you may want to give it a titbit. Ask your instructor first if it's OK and don't overdo it. A carrot or an apple is a healthy snack that will not expand its waistline!

Gaits

Humans can only walk or run, but a pony has four distinct ways of moving, called gaits. These are walk, trot, canter and gallop. As you progress, you'll certainly have a go at the first three and may one day even enjoy the thrill of a gallop!

Walk is the slowest of a pony's gaits. It is described as four-time because there are four beats to every stride. Watch a pony walk along and you'll see it places its hooves on the ground in the following order – near hind, near fore (front), off hind, near fore.

There are two beats to every stride in trot, which is why it's called a two-time gait. A pony springs from one diagonal pair of legs to the other, with a moment of suspension in between.

Canter is a three-time gait, with three beats to every stride followed by a moment of suspension when all four feet are off the ground. The foreleg that moves on its own is called the leading leg and a pony can lead with either its right or left foreleg. The sequence is: either hindleg first, the other hindleg and its diagonal fore together, the remaining foreleg.

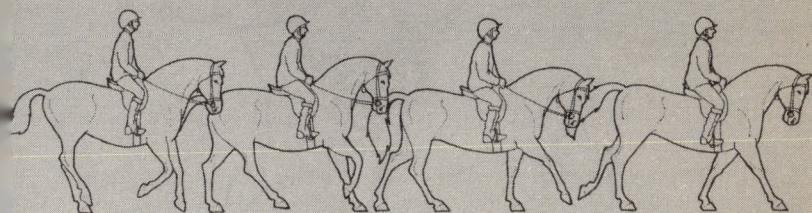

Gallop is the fastest of a pony's gaits. It's a four-time pace with four beats to every stride followed by a pause when all four feet are off the ground. A pony moves its legs in this order: either hindleg, then the other hindleg, the diagonal foreleg, then the remaining foreleg.

6 | Into trot

Be prepared for a bumpy ride! The trot is a pony's bounciest gait. The reason it feels so different to walk is because it is two-time. Instead of lifting one foot off the ground at a time, a pony springs from one pair of diagonal feet to the other. The good news is you'll find it a lot more comfortable when you have learnt to rise up and down in the saddle, in time with your pony's movement.

Rising trot

Rise to the trot correctly and you'll avoid a sore bottom and a grumpy pony. The idea's simple – you lift your seat slightly out of the saddle on the 'up' beat and then sit gently back down on the 'down' beat. Practise rising when the pony is standing still first and you'll find it easier when you try it for real in trot.

54

Look ahead and try to stay in balance with your pony.

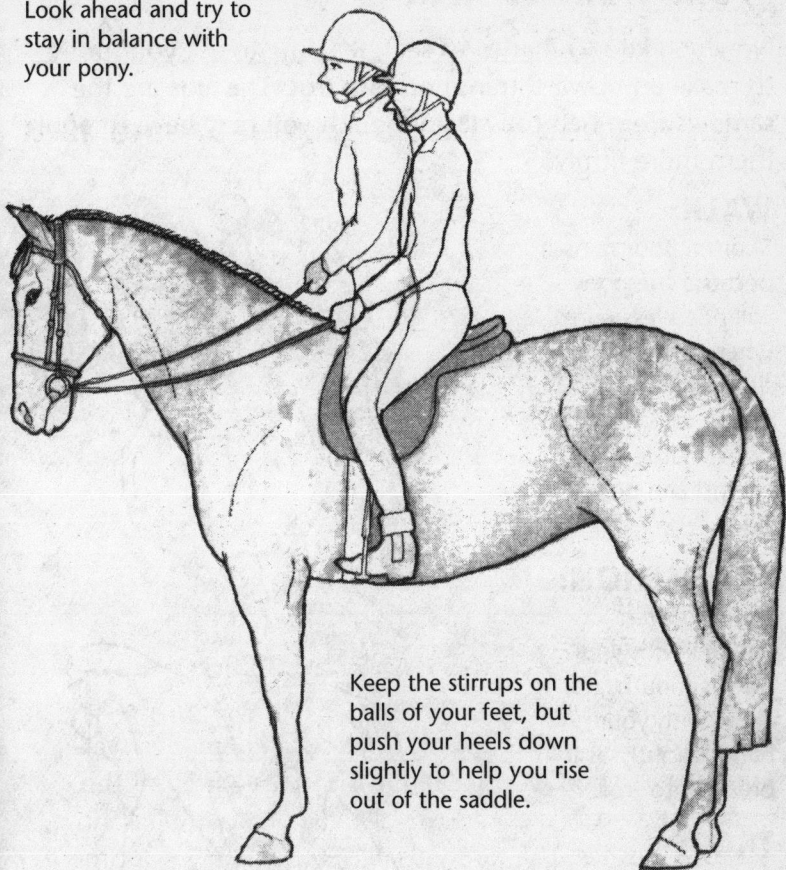

Keep the stirrups on the balls of your feet, but push your heels down slightly to help you rise out of the saddle.

Practising rising trot at halt.

Beat it!

If you have trouble sticking to a rhythm in rising trot, or if your pony tends to rush along, count out a rhythm. Say to yourself, 'up, down, up, down' or 'one, two, one, two'. You'll soon pick up the beat and settle into a steady pace.

From walk to trot

Now you know what to expect, it's time to ask your pony to make an upward transition into trot. The aids are the same as from halt to walk, although you may have to apply them more firmly.

WALK:

Shorten your reins, because the pony will need less rein when it is trotting, sit up tall in the saddle and squeeze both your legs against the pony's sides.

TRANSITION:

Keep an even contact with your pony's mouth, but allow with your hands slightly as it breaks into trot.

TROT:

Sit for a few strides to get your balance, then have a go at rising. Keep your legs wrapped around your pony's sides, but squeeze only if you want to go faster or if you feel your pony slowing down. Keep your hands as still as possible.

From trot to walk

After a circuit of the manege in trot, you'll probably be begging your instructor to let you go back to walk. That's OK – a few strides of trot is plenty to begin with. Don't just collapse in a heap. Relax and ask your pony for a smooth transition. First, stop rising for a few strides. Sit tall and deep in the saddle and apply gentle pressure on the reins – not too much, though, because you don't want to stop dead! As soon as your pony walks, release the pressure and get your breath back.

Quick quiz
Oops!

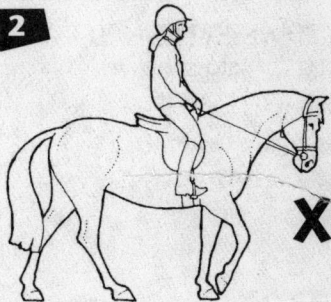

These three riders all want their ponies to make a downward transition from trot to walk – but they're not having much luck. Can you see what each one is doing wrong? You'll find the answers over the page.

Quick quiz

ANSWERS

1 This rider has tensed up and is gripping with her knees to try to stay on board. She wants to slow down, but her legs have slipped backwards. Her pony thinks she wants to go faster!

2 No wonder this pony looks confused. Its rider has forgotten to stop rising out of the saddle when asking for a transition into walk.

3 This rider has tipped forwards, which is a common rider problem. Taking her weight out of the saddle and looking down has made the pony speed up, not slow down.

Try to relax and sit tall when making a transition.

All change!

As explained earlier, in rising trot you rise and sit as your pony springs from one diagonal pair of legs to the other. But how do you know which pair to rise to?

Well, as your pony's outside foreleg (the one furthest from the centre of the school) comes back, you should be sitting. When it moves forwards, you should rise. This means that you have to 'change your diagonal' every time you change the rein (ride in the opposite direction). To do this, simply sit down for an extra beat as you cross the centre of the manege. Instead of going 'up, down, up, down', go 'up, down, down, up'. Riding on the correct diagonal is more comfortable for you and will help your pony stay supple and balanced.

Change your diagonal by sitting in the saddle for two beats, instead of one.

Test yourself

Next time you go into rising trot, see if you can tell, just by feel, whether you're riding on the correct diagonal. Glance down at your pony's outside shoulder to see if you're right. Practise until you're right every time.

Sitting pretty

Sitting to the trot is another way of riding this gait. It gives you a much closer contact with your pony, but takes a lot of practice. You must relax, look ahead and absorb all the bounces through your knees and hips.

Sitting trot will help you:
- Improve your balance and develop an 'independent seat'. This means you won't be relying on the reins and stirrups for support.
- Make a transition into or out of trot and canter.
- Eventually ride more advanced movements.

Did you know?

Highly trained horses and ponies can perform four types of trot – collected, working, medium and extended. In collected trot, the strides are high and short; in extended trot they're lengthened to cover as much ground as possible. The other two types are in between.

In extended trot, a horse looks as if it's floating across the ground.

Help!

Q No matter how hard I try, I feel as if I'm about to fall off my pony in trot. What can I do?

A Practise, practise and practise! Most riders find trot tricky at first, but there are a couple of things that will make you feel more secure. Ask your instructor if you can have some lessons on the lungeing rein. The instructor will attach a long rein to a special piece of tack called a lunge cavesson and use this to tell the pony when to trot, walk and stop. This will allow you to concentrate on your position without having to worry about controlling your pony. If you find you bump about, hold the pommel with one hand. You could also ask your instructor to a put a neckstrap on your pony. This will give you something to grab hold of if you start to lose your balance.

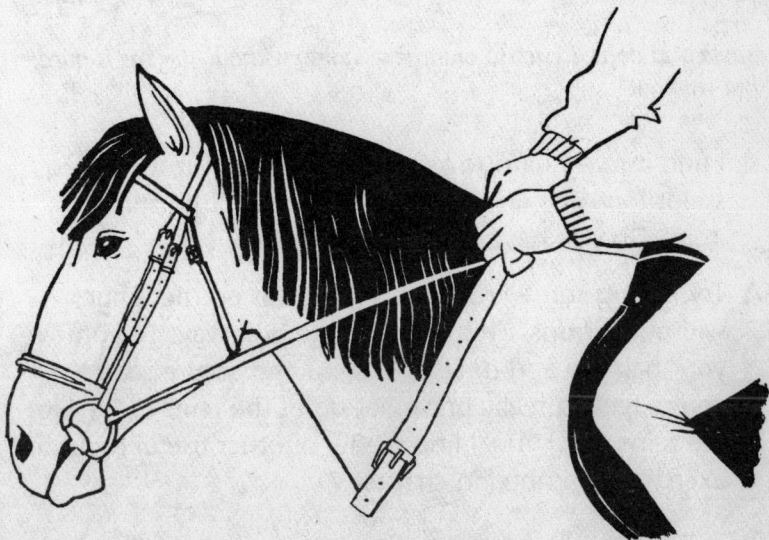

If you lose your balance, hold a neckstrap.

61

Smile and don't forget to breathe – riding without stirrups is hard, but worth it!

Q I find it really hard to keep my position in trot. My legs shoot forwards and my feet slip through the stirrup irons. Do you have any suggestions?

A Try having some lessons in sitting trot on the lunge, without stirrups. This is one of the best ways to improve your balance and develop a deep and secure seat. If you're feeling really brave, let go of the reins too. (Knot the reins first.) You'll find plenty of other useful mounted exercises described in chapter 7.

When you do take your stirrups back, ask your instructor to check they're the right length. They might be too long, which is why your feet are slipping through the irons.

A sharp tap with a whip will soon wake up a lazy pony.

Q The pony I have lessons on is so lazy. I can manage to keep it going for only a couple of strides in trot and then it stops. How can I wake it up?

A It sounds as if you've drawn the short straw and ended up on the riding school's Mr Plod. You could ask for a different pony, but you'll become a better rider in the long run if you stick with old slow-coach. Make sure your leg aids are clear and if the pony doesn't listen, repeat them more strongly. Still ignoring you? Then give it a sharp smack with your whip. That should get its attention and you can drive it forwards into an energetic trot. Use your legs to keep it going, but remember that an occasional sharp nudge in its sides is better than flapping about continuously.

7 Shape up

MOUNTED EXERCISES • RIDER FITNESS

Your pony may be supple, toned and full of beans, but what about you? You don't need to be a top-class athlete to ride well, but it's a lot more fun if you can trot without having to stop and catch your breath every few strides. There's nothing like a few mounted exercises or a quick work-out to make you feel more at home and confident in the saddle.

Balancing act

Mounted exercises in halt, walk or trot are one of the best ways to improve your balance, suppleness and position in the saddle. They can either be performed on the lunge, with your instructor controlling your pony, or at halt with a helper holding it. Always do these exercises in an enclosed space on a quiet pony who won't be upset if you accidentally knock or bump its sides.

Take 'em away!

You'll hear your instructor telling you to 'Quit and cross your stirrups'. This means take your feet out of the irons and cross the leathers in front of the saddle, left over right. You cross them in this order in case you fall off – you'll need to get at your left stirrup first in order to get back on! It's also a good idea to tie a knot in your reins to stop them getting in your way.

Leg lift

Grab your left ankle with your right hand and draw your foot back and up behind you. Then lower your leg and do the same with your right foot. This will help loosen your thigh muscles and get your legs in the correct position.

Touch your toes

This is hard enough when you're not on a pony, but give it a go because it'll help make your waist supple. Fold forwards and reach down with your right hand to touch your left toes. Sit up again then bend down to touch your right toes with your left hand.

Do the twist

This exercise is good for strengthening your upper body. Raise both arms to shoulder height and slowly twist your body from left to right.

Arm circling

Rotate your arms
backwards or forwards,
singly or together in
both directions. The
choice is yours!

Poll position

Stretch forwards to touch
your pony's poll with your
right hand. Sit up and
repeat the exercise using
your left hand.

Lean back

If you're feeling very brave,
try this one. Lean
backwards until your
shoulders and head are
resting on your pony's
rump. No cheating – you
must keep your legs in the
correct riding position
throughout the exercise!

67

Work it out!

To ride to the best of your ability, you need strength and stamina. So pull on your tracksuit bottoms and work those muscles – your pony won't believe it's the same rider!

Getting warm

It's important to warm up before any type of exercise. Walk up and down the stairs, jog on the spot or do some gentle stretching. Repeat this routine to cool down afterwards, too.

On your bike

Aerobic exercise is what you need to improve your overall fitness. Running, swimming and cycling will all do the trick!

Shoulders and arms

Get down on your hands and knees with your hands facing forwards. Keep your back straight and slowly bend your elbows until your nose is almost touching the floor. Return to the start position and repeat the exercise.

Legs

Lie on your left side, with your left arm bent at the elbow to support yourself. Keep your left leg straight and your right leg bent at the knee behind it. Slowly raise your left leg until your ankle is a few centimetres off the ground. Hold the position for a few seconds, then lower your leg to the floor. Repeat and then swap sides to work your right leg.

Stomach

Lie with your back flat on the floor, your knees bent and your hands gently supporting the sides of your head. Keep your feet hip width apart. Raise your shoulders off the ground a few centimetres, hold the position for a few seconds and then gently lower yourself back down. You'll have a super-toned tummy in no time!

Celeb fitness secrets

- Olympic three-day eventer Karen Dixon jogs to stay in shape.
- Showjumper Guy Goosen likes nothing better than a round of golf.
- It's alright for some... Tennis player Martina Hingis is already super-fit. Riding's her one chance to relax!

Record-breakers

TALLEST, SMALLEST, HAIRIEST OR FASTEST – THEY'RE ALL EQUINE SUPERSTARS

A racing legend

Bay gelding Red Rum raced into the history books by winning the Grand National an awesome three times. He was also runner-up twice.

The pocket-sized pony

Tiny skewbald miniature horse Countess Natuschka is officially the smallest horse in the world. The Guinness Book of Records recently measured her height as 6.3hh (68.5 cm) – roughly the same size as a large dog!

An equine granddad

Old Billy is possibly the world's oldest-ever horse. Born in Lancashire, UK, in 1760, he lived to the ripe old age of 62.

Pass the ladder...

One of the tallest horses on record is a Shire gelding called Sampson (later re-named Mammoth) who was born in 1846. He stood a neck-achingly tall 21.2½hh (2.2 metres).

Into orbit

Chilean Captain Alberto Morales must have seen stars in 1949 when he and his horse Huaso cleared a jump measuring 2.44 metres. No-one has yet beaten this record.

A Derby first

Brave 14.2hh (1.47 metres) pony Stroller is the only pony ever to have won the British Hickstead Derby. He took on the famous bank and devil's dyke to snatch victory in 1967, with his rider Marion Coakes (now Mould).

Tell-tail

The longest tail ever recorded belonged to stunning 15hh (1.52 metres) palomino Belvedere Forest King from Canada. When unbraided, it measured a hairy 6.7 metres. Not to be outdone, a horse called Maud, from California, USA, had a mane 5.5 metres long.

Baby love

A 42-year-old Australian mare astonished her owners in 1933 when she gave birth to a record 34th foal.

Fast forward

CANTER • YOUR POSITION • THE AIDS
• COPING WITH PROBLEMS

Picking up speed is exciting and most ponies love a good canter as much as their riders. Unlike trot, it's a comfy, rhythmic, rocking pace – so sit back and enjoy the ride!

TROT:

Before you ask your pony to canter, make sure it's moving forwards with plenty of impulsion in trot, but not too fast. Take sitting trot for a few strides, then squeeze your inside leg on the girth. At the same time, bring your outside leg behind the girth and give a firm nudge.

Ask for canter by bringing your outside leg slightly behind the girth.

TRANSITION:

You should feel a little bounce as your pony strikes off into canter. If not, don't just trot faster and faster. Either immediately back up your leg aids with the whip or steady up into a balanced trot and try again.

CANTER:

There are three beats to every stride in canter. Count '1, 2, 3... 1, 2, 3' to yourself. This will help you to establish a calm, balanced rhythm.

HEAD: It's extra-important to look where you're going in canter, because everything happens much more quickly than in walk or trot.

HANDS: Your pony will move its head and neck quite a lot in canter. Keep a steady contact with its mouth, but allow your hands to follow this movement.

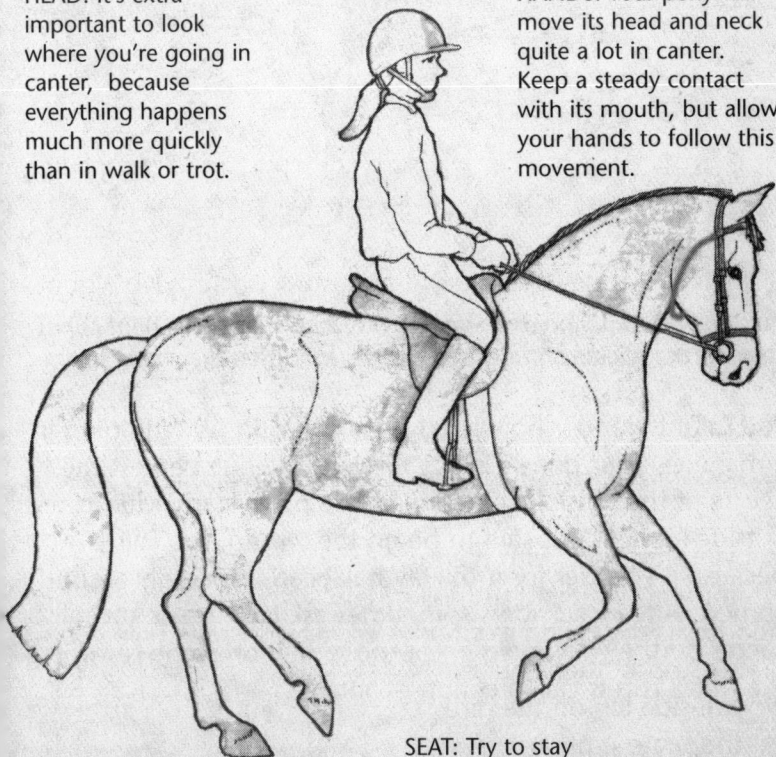

LEGS: Keep your legs close to your pony's sides. Be ready to push on if your pony starts to slow down or tries to break into trot.

SEAT: Try to stay supple through your hips and back and sit deep and tall in the saddle. If you tense up, it'll be uncomfortable for you and your pony.

Right or wrong?

X

This pony is cantering on the right rein which means the right rein is towards the middle of the school. However, it is on the wrong leg.

You might wonder how a leg can be wrong. When riding in a manege, your pony's inside foreleg (the one nearest the centre of the school) should lead. If a pony leads with its outside foreleg, it is said to be on the wrong leg. This is because it's harder for it to stay balanced, especially around corners. Advanced riders sometimes ask their horse to canter on the wrong leg on purpose, in a dressage test for example. This is called counter-canter.

If you are cantering your pony on the right rein (with the right rein towards the centre of the school), it should lead with its right foreleg. On the left rein, it should lead with its left foreleg.

You can check you've got it right by quickly glancing down at your pony's front legs. You'll be able to see which one is stretching forwards the most. Learn to feel which leg your pony is cantering on so you don't have to look down.

Watch those corners!

The aids for riding turns and circles in canter are the same as in any other gait. Ask your pony to bend around your inside leg and use your inside rein to guide it into the turn. Your outside hand controls your pony's speed while your outside leg stays behind the girth to stop its quarters from swinging out.

Canter to trot

When making a downward transition from canter to trot, sit tall and deep in the saddle. Squeeze your reins to tell your pony to slow down, but don't just collapse into trot. Be ready to use your legs to keep your pony moving forwards after the transition.

When cantering on a circle, ask your pony to bend around your inside leg.

Problem

I can't sit still in the saddle when my pony canters. How can I stop myself from bouncing around so much?

Solution

Try this exercise: In canter, put both reins into your outside hand and hold the back of the saddle with your inside hand. This will help you to move with your pony and keep your bottom in the saddle.

Problem

I keep losing my stirrups in canter. Help!

Solution

Unless your stirrups are too long, this probably happens because you feel tense and start to grip with your knees. You might think this will help you to stay in the saddle but, in fact, you're more likely to lose your stirrups and bounce off. If you don't fancy going into orbit, try to relax and stay calm. Bring your pony back to walk, put your feet back into the stirrups and have another go.

Problem

My pony often strikes off on the wrong leg when I ask it to canter. What can I do?

Solution

Always ask for canter in a corner of the school or on a circle. You could also use your inside rein to encourage your pony to bend to the inside through its head and neck. This will help it stay balanced and make it easier to strike off on the correct leg. Remember to keep your inside leg on the girth and your outside leg slightly behind it. If things go wrong, simply come back to trot and ask for canter again at the next corner.

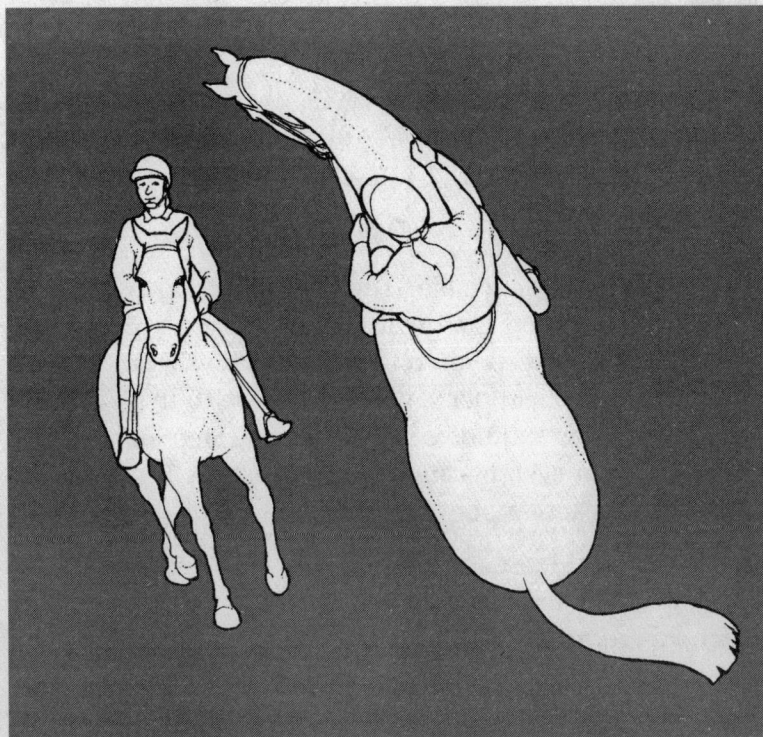

If things go wrong in canter, come back to trot and try again.

9 | Join the gang

RIDING IN A GROUP LESSON
• SCHOOL EXERCISES

Fed up with the single life? Then have a group lesson. Riding with others is a great way to improve your skills and it'll certainly keep you on your toes. As well as controlling your own pony, you'll also have to think about the other ponies and riders in your lesson. Steering's more important than ever, because your instructor will not be happy if you cause a pony pile-up!

Get away!

Now you're in a group there's no excuse for sloppy riding. It's up to you to control your pony and avoid collisions with the other riders in your lesson. Think ahead and remember the A, B, C of riding school rules.

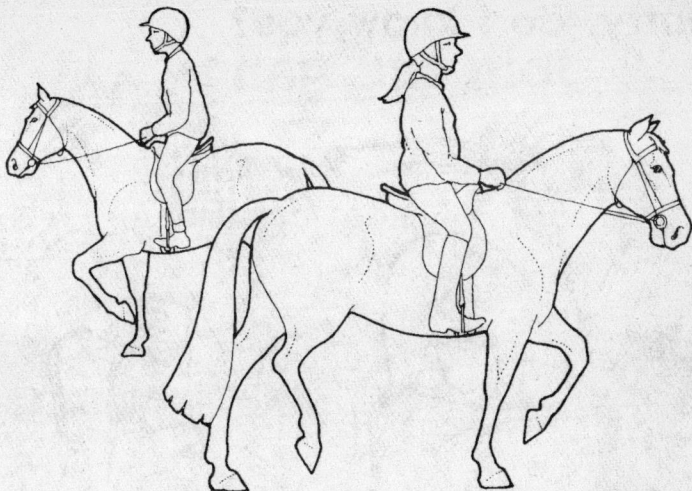

Always pass other riders left hand to left hand, when riding in opposite directions around the school.

Be aware of where other riders are in the school. Don't stop suddenly, or you could catch them by surprise! If you want to alter your stirrups, halt in the centre of the school out of everybody's way. If you are walking when other people are trotting, keep to the inside track.

Circle away if you get too close to the pony in front of you – otherwise it may kick out. Aim to keep at least a pony's length between you and the rider in front.

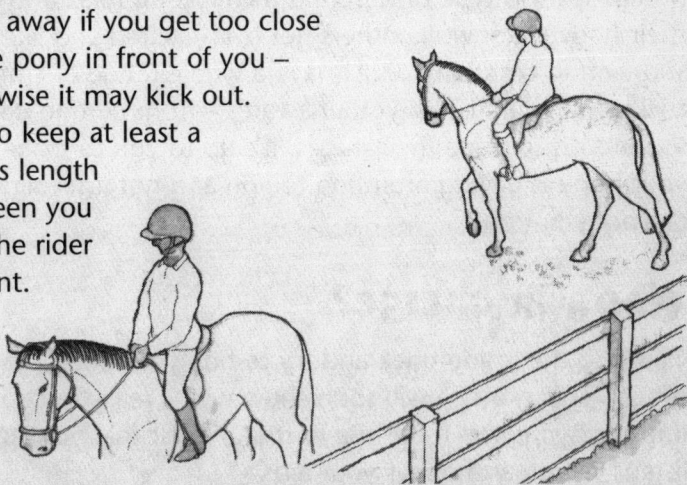

Sorry, do I know you?

Don't be surprised if your pony behaves differently in a group and shows a whole new side to its character. Some ponies see this type of lesson as a chance to relax and put their hooves up, while others get over-excited and like to show-off in company. Most have a whole range of crafty tricks that could catch you unawares – from cutting corners to refusing to leave their mates. It's up to you to make sure your pony is paying attention to you and not just following the pony in front.

Who's in charge?

Come to the inside track and try to ride your pony past the others. This exercise will soon show who's really in control. If it's not you, sort it out! Be firm and insist that your pony listens to you and obeys your aids.

Top tip

At the beginning of a lesson, your instructor may ask you to warm up your pony 'in open order'. This means you can ride wherever you like in the school, as long as you don't bump into anyone else. It's a good opportunity to get your pony listening to you by doing simple transitions and turns in walk and trot on both reins.

The arena

Look around the edge of the school and you'll spot markers with the letters A, K, E, H, C, M, B and F. Your instructor will use these letters to tell the ride where to start a new movement. There's also an imaginary letter, X, which is in the centre of the school. Remember the sentence '**A**ll **K**ing **E**dward's **H**orses **C**an **M**anage **B**ig **F**ences' and you'll have no problem finding your way around.

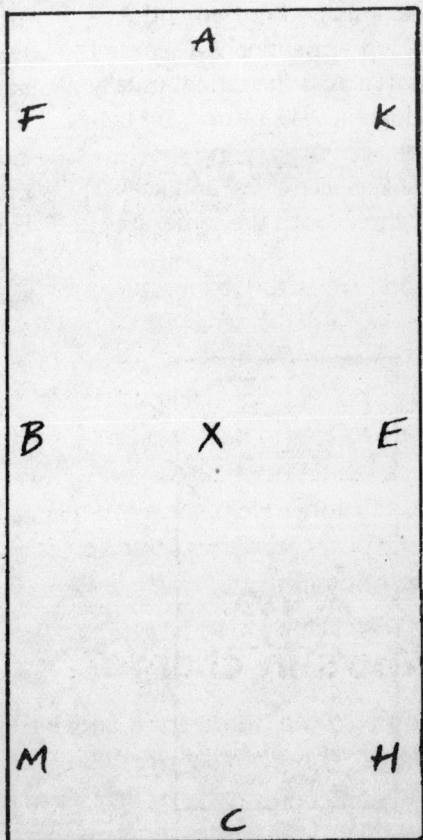

A
F   K
B   X   E
M   H
C

81

Back to school

Forget geography and history, because this is homework for horses! School movements will help your pony stay supple and obedient to your aids. They are also a good test of your riding skills. There are loads of different movements to choose from, and most can be ridden as a group or 'in succession' (one after another). Here are a few your instructor might ask you to try.

3-loop serpentine

Not a type of snake, but a snake-shaped movement! A 3-loop serpentine is a series of turns across the school usually ridden in walk or trot. Try to ride accurately, using the markers as guides, and keep all three loops the same size.

Circles

These can be either 20, 15 or 10 metres in size. Fifteen and twenty-metre circles are the easiest and are usually ridden from A, B, E or C. Ten-metre circles are a lot harder and are usually ridden in one of the corners of the school.

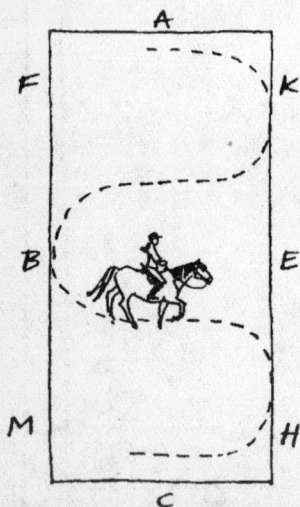

Changing the rein

This means changing the direction in which you're riding. The easiest ways to do this are:

1 Ride diagonally across the school, eg from M to K, and then turn to go around the school on the other rein.
2 Turn across the centre of the school eg from E to B.
3 Turn down the centre line eg from A to C.

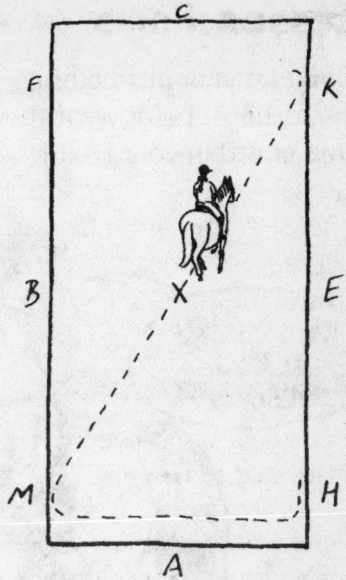

Figure of eight

This is basically two 20-metre circles joined together. It's harder than it looks because of all the changes in direction and bend you must do.

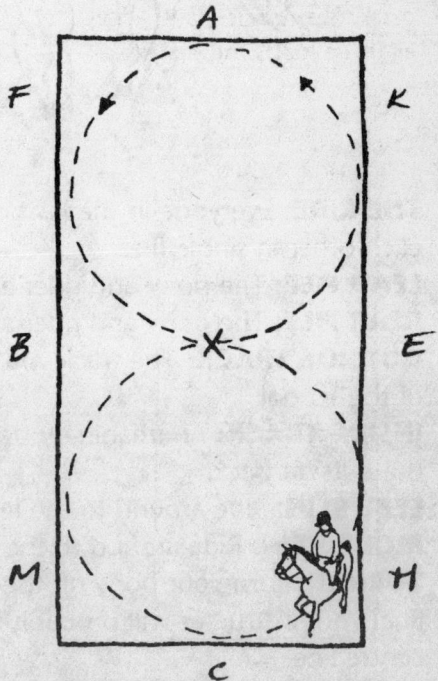

Lesson lingo

Don't let your instructor confuse you with strange-sounding instructions. Learn what they *really* mean and you'll be one step ahead in your next lesson.

WHAT'S SHE TALKING ABOUT?

DON'T ASK ME!

THE RIDE: Everyone in the lesson. Riders usually follow each other in single file.

LEAD FILE: The pony and rider at the front of the ride.

REAR FILE: The pony and rider at the back of the ride.

OUTSIDE TRACK: The track you ride around at the edge of the school.

INSIDE TRACK: An imaginary track about 5 metres in from the outside track.

LEFT REIN: Ride around to the left.

RIGHT REIN: Ride around to the right.

TURN IN: Turn your pony off the track towards the centre line. Your instructor will probably ask you to halt on the centre line.

KEEP YOUR DISTANCE: Reminds riders to keep a pony's length between them and the rider in front. Don't get too close or lag behind.

PREPARE TO... A warning that your instructor is about to ask you to change pace or direction or start a new movement. It gives you a chance to warn your pony too.

CHANGE THE REIN: Change the direction in which you're riding.

GO LARGE: Go around the school on the outside track.

CENTRE LINE: An imaginary line straight down the centre of the school between the markers A and C.

Speak up!

Don't be afraid to ask a question if you don't understand something. Your instructor will be happy to explain it to you. That's what he or she is there for!

Pony care

GROOMING • FEEDING • MUCKING OUT

All ponies need a daily routine that keeps them fit, healthy and happy. Looking after a pony can be as much fun as riding – and there's lots to learn.

Get grooming

Grooming removes dirt from a pony's coat, improves circulation and helps tone the muscles. Don't overdo it on a grass-kept pony because it needs some natural grease in its coat to protect it in bad weather.

THE GROOMING KIT

Dandy brush for removing mud and stable stains.

Body brush for brushing the whole pony and mane and tail.

Water brush for scrubbing the feet, washing off stains and laying the mane and tail flat.

Mane comb for combing the mane.

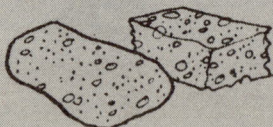

Hoof pick for cleaning out the feet.

Sponges for cleaning the eyes, nose and dock.

Sweat scraper for removing water from the coat.

Metal curry comb for cleaning the body brush.

Rubber curry comb for removing mud.

For safety, always tie a pony up using a quick-release knot

Grub's up!

Eating is a pony's favourite hobby after sleeping. Most horses and ponies need two types of feed in their diet – roughage, such as grass or hay, plus energy-giving food such as oats or barley. The amount a pony needs depends on its size and the amount of work it's doing. All ponies need a constant supply of fresh water.

Home sweet home

Ponies spend most of their time in a field or stable, so it's important to keep these places clean. A stabled pony must be mucked out daily, which is when you remove all the droppings and add new bedding (usually straw or shavings or sometimes paper). You must remove droppings from the field too.

FACTFILE

- All ponies need their hooves trimmed regularly by a farrier.
- Ponies should have their teeth rasped twice a year by a vet or horse dentist.

Jump to it!

THE STAGES OF A JUMP
• JUMPING POSITION • YOUR FIRST FENCE
• TACKLING A COURSE

A pony's jump feels a bit like like an extra-big, bouncy canter stride so if you're confident in canter, you'll have no worries going airborne. If you're a bit nervous about tackling your first jump, spare a thought for competitors in the puissance showjumping classes. A huge red wall goes higher and higher until only one horse clears it and is the winner. The wall regularly goes up to more than 2 metres – that's taller than most people!

Your stirrups

When you jump a fence, you must lean forwards to stay in balance with your pony. This is much easier if you ride with your stirrups a couple of holes shorter than your normal riding length.

Jumping Position

BACK: As your
pony takes off,
fold forwards from
your hips, keeping
your back straight.

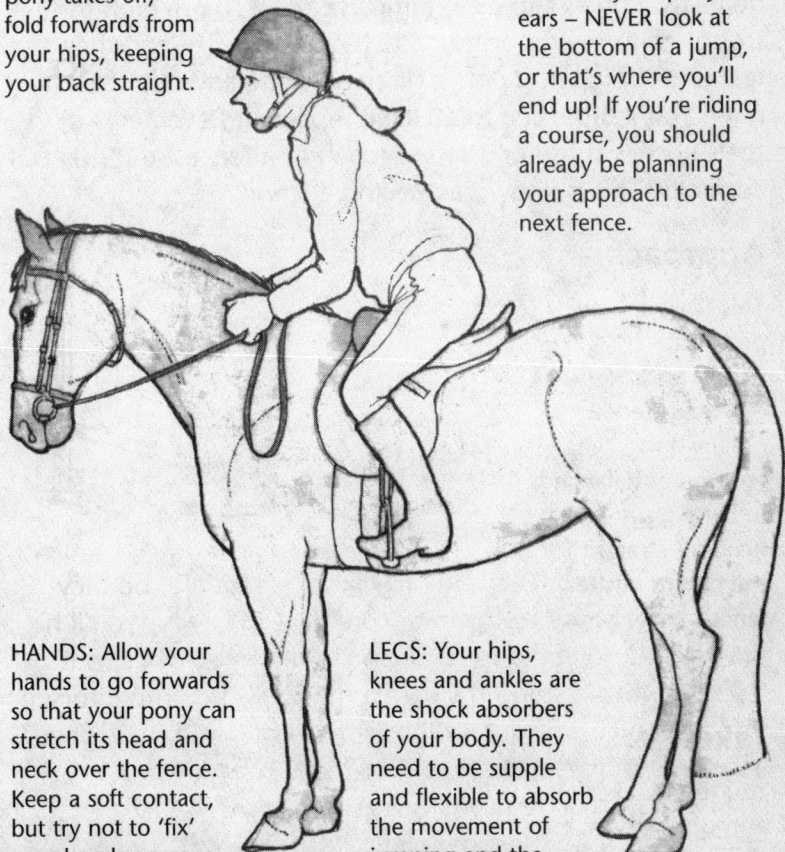

HEAD: Keep your head
up, and look straight
between your pony's
ears – NEVER look at
the bottom of a jump,
or that's where you'll
end up! If you're riding
a course, you should
already be planning
your approach to the
next fence.

HANDS: Allow your
hands to go forwards
so that your pony can
stretch its head and
neck over the fence.
Keep a soft contact,
but try not to 'fix'
your hands on your
pony's neck.

LEGS: Your hips,
knees and ankles are
the shock absorbers
of your body. They
need to be supple
and flexible to absorb
the movement of
jumping and the
impact on landing.

*Practise your jumping position in halt, walk, trot and
canter. Aim to stay in balance with your pony, without
resting your hands on its neck or hanging on the
reins. Hold the mane if you like, or ask to have a
neckstrap on to which you can hang.*

How a pony jumps

A pony's jump can be divided into five different stages: approach, take-off, moment of suspension, landing and getaway. Ponies can clear jumps nearly 1 metre high from trot or canter without much help from their rider. When the fences get bigger, a pony will need some advice from its rider. You'll often see top showjumpers and eventers adjust their horse's stride on the approach to a fence, so it meets it correctly. This is known as 'seeing a stride'.

Approach:

This is when your pony sizes up the height and position of the fence. Sit quietly and keep your pony balanced, full of energy and heading straight for the centre of the fence.

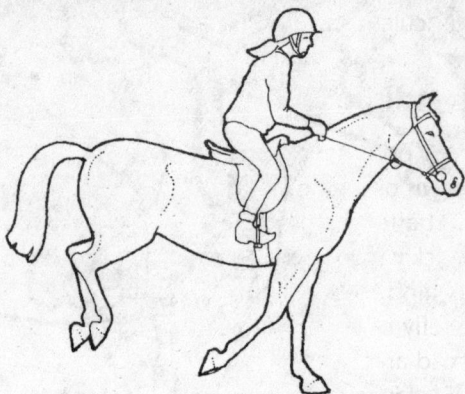

Take-off:

Your pony takes off at roughly the same distance away from a fence as its height. It raises its head and propels itself into the air off its powerful hocks.

Moment of suspension:

Don't look down! Your pony has all four feet off the ground now, as it stretches its head and neck forwards, tucks up its legs and rounds its back. This shape is known as a 'bascule'.

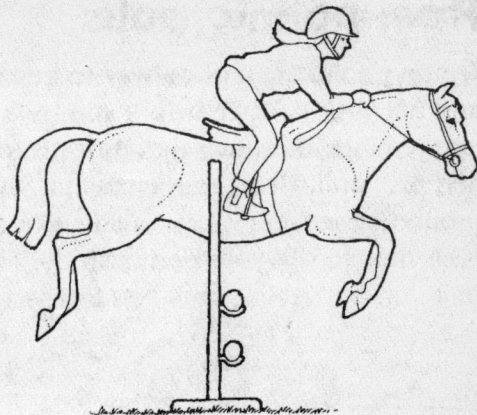

Landing:

Your pony touches down on one fore-foot after the other, quickly followed by its hind feet. It then briefly raises its head and neck to re-balance itself.

Getaway:

After landing, push your pony forwards in a straight line away from the fence. It's important to re-establish your rhythm as quickly as possible – especially if you're riding around a course.

From pole to pole

Trotting poles are a good way to build up your confidence and get your balance before you try a proper jump. They'll also remind your pony that it needs to look where it's going and pick up its feet! Your instructor will lay poles on the ground either singly, or in a line with a distance between each pole to suit your pony's stride. Trot your pony over the poles on both reins, until you feel secure.

When setting up a line of trotting poles, remember that one of your pony's strides is about the same as two of your walking ones.

Pole pointers

- Aim for the centre of the line of poles.
- Use your legs to keep your pony moving forwards – if it falls asleep, it'll trip up!
- Ride the exercise in rising trot, sitting trot and jumping position.
- Once you're confident in trot, your instructor may turn the poles into canter poles by removing every other one from the line. When you ride through in canter you'll feel your pony lift its head, neck and forelegs and bounce over each pole. This is the same feeling you'll get over a jump.

Prepare for take-off...

Fasten your seatbelt and hold tight, because this is the moment of truth. The next step is to add a very small cross-pole to the end of your line of trotting poles. Ride down the centre of the poles as before, but this time fold forwards from your hips and allow with your hands as your pony pops over the jump. Easy!

Get into grids

Don't ride though the same grid again and again, or your pony will become fed-up and grumpy!

A row of poles and jumps on the ground is called a grid. In gridwork, the distance between fences is carefully measured so your pony will meet each fence correctly. This builds up its confidence and allows you to concentrate on your position. There are many different types of grid and they can be built with no strides between fences called a bounce, or with one or more canter strides between each jump. This type of jumping is hard work for both you and your pony, so sessions should be short to start with.

How NOT to do it!

Recognise yourself? If so, you're in good company because even top showjumpers have off-days, when everything seems to go wrong. There are all sorts of reasons for this, ranging from rider faults to a pony that's in pain, afraid or plain naughty. Here are a few of the most common problems.

PROBLEM: Refusal

WHY IT HAPPENS: ▶
Usually because the pony didn't think you were that keen to go over! Be honest now, were you feeling a teeny bit worried about the size of the fence?

X

SOLUTION:
Be positive. Ride strongly into the fence, convinced you'll get over. Give your pony every chance of clearing it by riding straight for the centre of the jump. It should sense your confidence and clear it well.

PROBLEM: Getting 'left behind'

WHY IT HAPPENS: Pony takes off before you're ready.

SOLUTION: If this happens to you, quickly slip the reins through your fingers so you don't jab your pony in the mouth. Next time, fold forwards into your jumping position earlier, so you stay in balance.

PROBLEM: Running-out

WHY IT HAPPENS: Often because you made a bad approach to the fence.

SOLUTION: Make sure you aim for the centre of the jump. If your pony always tends to duck out to one particular side, swap your whip into that hand and shorten your opposite rein, ready to straighten it.

PROBLEM: Fixed hands

WHY IT HAPPENS: You're not allowing your hands to follow your pony's movement.

SOLUTION: Practise moving your hands further up your pony's neck in trot and canter. Remember it's more likely to clear the fence if you allow it to stretch forwards over it.

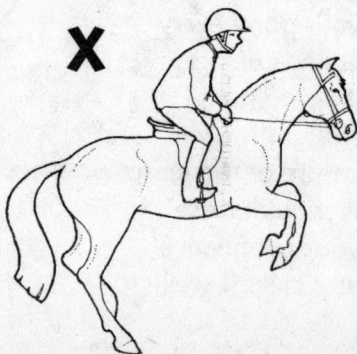

PROBLEM: Knock-down

WHY IT HAPPENS: ▶

A poor approach, your pony being careless or over-faced (the jump was too big).

SOLUTION: Give your pony plenty of room to turn and approach the fence. If it's being lazy, give it a tap with your whip. Lower the jump if necessary.

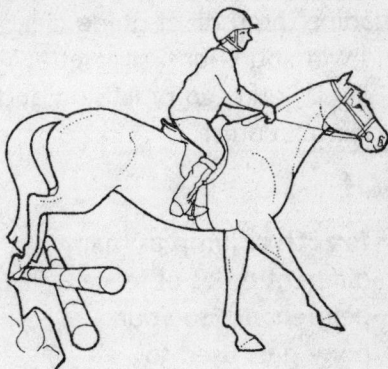

X

PROBLEM: Legs too far back

◀

WHY IT HAPPENS:

Perhaps you're gripping up with your knees in an attempt to stay on, or your stirrup leathers may be too long.

SOLUTION: Check your stirrup length and try to relax. If your legs swing too far back, you'll be less secure and could end up clearing the fence all by yourself!

X

Right on course

Imagine the thrill of going clear in a jumping competition and winning your first rosette. Your dream could become reality if you keep practising and follow these tips for tackling a course.

DO!

- **Practise.** Jump as many different types of fence beforehand, so your pony gets used to strange-looking fences.
- **Be positive.** Confidence is everything when it comes to jumping. You can do it!
- **Think ahead.** Walk the course on foot so you know where you need to turn your pony to make a good approach into each fence. Memorise the course so you don't go the wrong way.

DON'T!

- **Rush.** Concentrate on making wide turns into the fences, so your pony stays balanced and has plenty of time to suss out each jump.
- **Just sit there.** Most ponies enjoy jumping, but you'll need to use your legs so your pony has enough spring in its stride to clear the fences.
- **Worry!** If you don't go clear, it doesn't matter. Just try your best and have fun – there's always another day.

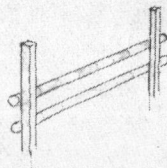

Good turns are the key to riding a course.

Types of jump

Visit a show and you'll see all sorts of different, brightly
coloured fences. They may be 'uprights', which means
they are fixed to a single set of jump wings, or 'spreads',
which are wider and built on two sets of wings.

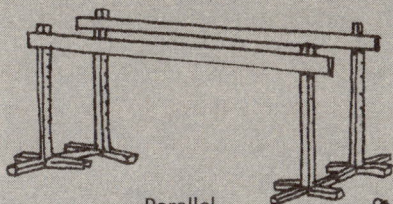

Parallel

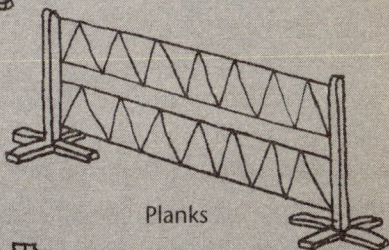

Planks

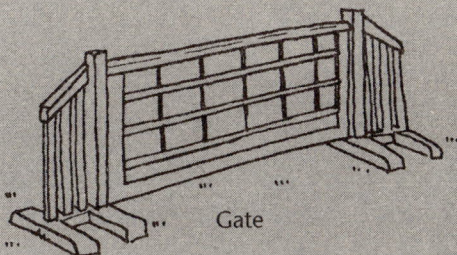

Gate

Staircase

Pony puzzlers

1 From which side is it usual to mount your pony?

2 What is the normal temperature of a healthy pony?

3

How many beats are there to every stride of gallop?

4 Metal and rubber are types of what?

5 What is an experienced pony often called?

6 What is the difference between an upright and a spread fence in showjumping?

7 A serpentine is a the name given to a row of poles on the ground – true or false?

8 Name two artificial aids.

9 Of the following words, which is the odd one out and why? Hay, straw, paper, shavings.

10 In trot, should you rise or sit when your pony's outside shoulder comes back?

100

11 For safety, what type of knot should you use when tying up a pony?

12 Using the stirrup to spring into the saddle is one way of mounting a pony. Name an alternative method?

13 When might you have to remember about King Edward's horses?

14 Name this tool. What is it used for?

15 What is a bascule?

16 Explain what 'offside' means when referring to a pony.

17 Before mounting, how can you check your stirrups are roughly the right length?

18 When cantering on the left rein, which of your pony's forelegs should 'lead'?

19 When you are riding, through which fingers do the reins pass?

20 In rising trot, how would you 'change the diagonal'?

• Now turn to page 122 to check your answers.

11 Can you hack it?

RIDING IN THE COUNTRY • ROAD SAFETY

Nothing beats seeing the countryside from horseback. Riding out, or hacking, is a fun alternative to a lesson, and your instructor will probably take you out and about as soon as you can control your pony in the school. You might even get the chance to go on special picnic rides or trips to the beach.

Tackling different terrain is exciting and your pony may feel more lively than usual. It's essential that you think ahead, listen to your instructor and use your common sense. Always wear a riding hat and bright or reflective clothes that are comfortable, safe, and easy for other road-users to spot.

Before you set off...

- Check your pony's tack is fitted correctly and in good condition.
- Tell someone where you're going and when you expect to be back.

Road sense

Most hacks involve riding on the road, so it's important that you know how to ride safely in traffic. It's best to ride in single file, keeping a pony's distance between you and the rider in front. Keep to the edge of the road, walking or trotting steadily in the same direction as other road-users.

The rider at the front, usually your instructor, will let you know when to speed up, slow down, stop and turn. The person at the rear, who should also be an experienced rider, will warn the ride that a car is behind and may tell the driver when it's safe to pass.

103

Coping with the unexpected

Your instructor will give you a quiet, traffic-proof pony to ride, but even the most sensible pony can sometimes take you by surprise! A pony that's unsure about a scary object, such as a flapping plastic bag, may shy and move sideways away from it. If this happens to you, stay calm and use your legs to ride your pony forwards strongly. Always carry your whip in your hand closest to the traffic, so you can ask your pony to move back to the edge of the road.

Sign language

You'll notice your instructor uses arm and hand signals to thank other road-users and warn them where the ride is going. Knowing what these signals mean will help you prepare your pony for a change in direction or pace.

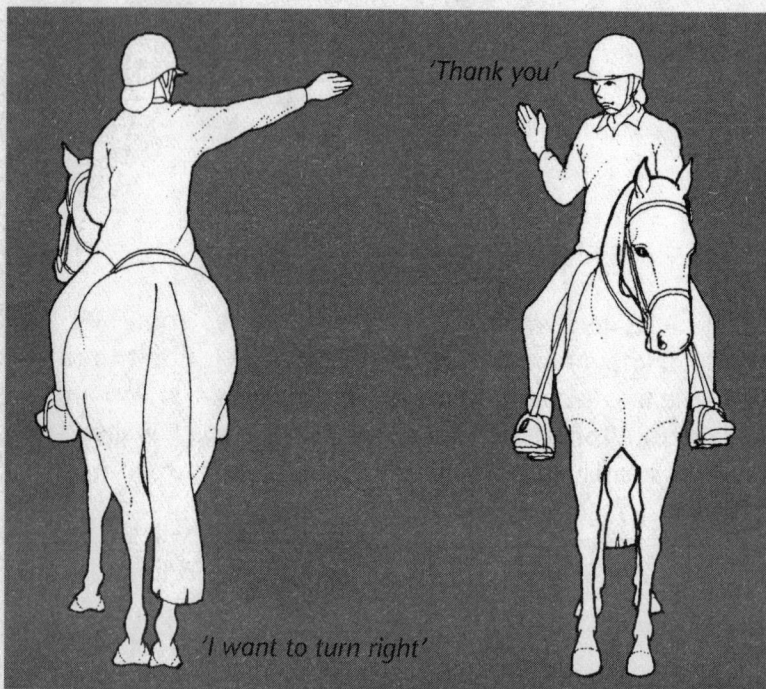

'Thank you'

'I want to turn right'

In the country

There are hundreds of fields and paths just waiting to be explored. Some of these will be perfect for a good canter and you may even find a small, fallen log to practise your jumping skills. Enjoy the scenery, but stay alert – a low branch can easily knock you out of the saddle if you're day-dreaming!

Up and down hill

Help your pony stay balanced by leaning back slightly when riding downhill and leaning forwards slightly when riding uphill.

Happy hacking

Follow these 10 golden rules to stay safe on the roads and in the countryside.

1. Be polite to everyone you meet – whether they're riders, walkers, cyclists or motorists.

2. Watch out for hazards such as rabbit holes, wire and ditches that could injure or trip up your pony.

3. Don't leave litter lying around.

4. Always close any gates behind you.

5. Give other road-users plenty of warning where you're going.

6. Know and understand the rules of the road. Obey traffic signs and road markings – they apply to riders as well as cars.

7. Walk quietly through fields that have herds of sheep, cows or other livestock in them.

8. Avoid riding when it's dark. If you have to ride at dusk or in bad weather, kit yourself and your pony out with reflective gear.

9. Always carry some money with you in case you need to phone for help in an emergency.

10. Don't trespass – stick to tracks where you know you are allowed to ride.

Going home

Follow this pony's tips to make sure your pony is as happy as you at the end of a hack.

Walk the last kilometre of a hack, to allow me to cool down.

Pick out my feet when we get home. There might be a stone stuck there.

Always check me over for any lumps, bumps, cuts or injuries.

When you untack me, use a body brush to remove any dried sweat marks on my coat.

Never let me gulp down bucketfuls of water straight after being ridden – it might give me colic. Let me have just a few mouthfuls and give me the rest once I've cooled down.

If it's a hot day, sponge me down with cool water because it is really refreshing.

12

Be a sport!

GET THE FACTS ABOUT HORSEY SPORTS FROM SHOWJUMPING TO POLO

Horses and ponies are as talented as humans when it comes to sport. They can turn their hooves to almost anything! You can learn loads watching famous horses and riders competing, so why not settle back, turn on the TV or video and improve your skills from the comfort of your own home. Seeing the stars in action may even inspire you to have a go at one of these sports yourself.

Showjumping

Ponies rarely jump in the wild unless they're fleeing from danger, but many have a natural talent for leaping skywards. Showjumpers compete against each other over a course of fences and incur faults for refusals, knock-downs and falls. Watch out for the world's top riders at the Sydney Olympics in Australia in the year 2000.

Showjumping fact!

Retired showjumper Milton, ridden by John Whitaker, was the first horse to win an awesome £1 million (UK) in prize-money.

Driving

From a leisurely drive in the country, to the fun of scurry racing or the challenge of driving cross-country, this is a fast-growing sport with something for everyone. You'll find competitions all over the world for singles, pairs and teams of horses.

Driving fact!

While many breeds are successfully used for driving, the Hackney, with its high-stepping action, is one of the most eye-catching.

Eventing

You need to be a good all-rounder to succeed in eventing, or horse trials. There are three phases to complete – dressage, speed and endurance (which includes roads and tracks, a steeplechase and cross-country), and showjumping. At the top level, New Zealand and Australian riders dominate the sport at the moment, closely followed by British, American and Irish. If you go to a big event, look out for stars such as Mark Todd (NZ), Matt Ryan (Aus) and Mary King (GB).

Eventing fact!

Britain's Lucinda Green (now retired) won the Badminton horse trials in England an incredible six times – on six different horses!

Flat racing

In Australia, flat racing is so popular that Melbourne Cup day is a national holiday. British and American fans aren't so lucky, but racing is big business in these countries too. Sleek, super-fit Thoroughbreds are the stars of the sport, but often jockeys are just as well known. Italian-born Frankie Dettori is a major crowd-puller and thrilled fans in Britain by becoming the first-ever jockey to win all seven races at one meeting.

Flat racing fact!

All Thoroughbred horses can trace their ancestry back to just three horses: The Byerly Turk, the Darley Arabian and the Godolphin Barb.

Steeplechasing

All the fun of flat racing, but with the added thrill of jumps! It's every jump-jockey's dream to win the British and Irish Grand Nationals, but no steeplechase in the world is tougher than Czechoslovakia's Pardubicka. This race is more than 6 kilometres long and there are 30 death-defying fences to jump.

Steeplechasing fact!

This sport took its name from early cross-country races, when riders raced from the steeple of one church to another.

Polo

A polo pony needs to be obedient, courageous – and fast.
These equine athletes reach speeds of about 65 km/h as
their riders try to hit the ball with their mallet, or stop rival
players hitting it. The game is played by two teams and
matches are divided into periods called 'chukkas', each
lasting seven and a half minutes.

Polo fact!

*Polo was first played in China and Persia about
2,500 years ago.*

Long-distance riding

This is a bit like running a marathon, but on horseback.
There are two types of long-distance competition. Horses
and riders compete in endurance rides over a set distance,
or in trail rides over a set distance at a stated speed.
Competitors need to be in tip-top physical and mental
condition to complete these events – some cover more than
160 km a day. Now that's what we call saddle-sore!

Long-distance fact!

Two famous long-distance events are the Golden Horseshoe in Britain and the Tom Quilty in Australia.

Dressage

Dressage horses are the ballerinas of the horse world. Controlled and graceful, they wow audiences worldwide as they perform difficult movements such as piaffe (trotting on the spot) and pirouettes (turns on the spot). German riders such as Nicole Uphoff-Becker are the ones to beat.

Dressage fact!

Nicole Uphoff-Becker is the youngest rider ever to win an Olympic gold medal in dressage. She was just 21 years old when she claimed her title in 1996, riding the bay gelding Rembrandt.

Harness racing

Australia, America, Russia and New Zealand are the places to visit if you want to catch some harness racing action. These are races for trotters (horses that trot normally, moving their legs in diagonal pairs) and pacers (horses that move their legs in lateral pairs – both nearside legs together then both offside legs together). A driver sits in a light, two-wheeled vehicle known as a sulky and guides the horse around the track as fast as possible. The winner is the horse that finishes first, without breaking out of its gait.

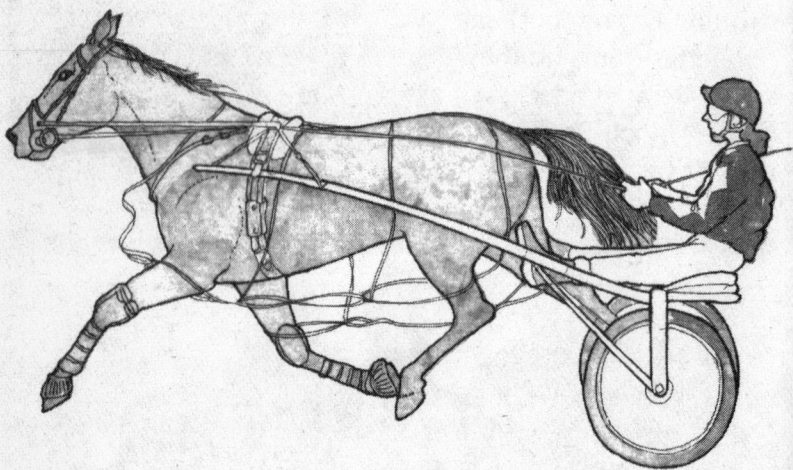

Harness racing fact!

One of the oldest equestrian sports, harness racing developed from ancient Greek and Roman chariot racing.

Fun 'n' games

Mounted games

Speed, accuracy and practice are what it takes to win in gymkhana games. Popular games include bending, musical poles, the sack race, and apple bobbing.

Horseball

A bit like netball on horseback, horseball is played with a football that has handles. Two teams of players try to gain possession of the ball and then pass it between themselves before throwing it through a hoop to score a goal.

Vaulting

This sport is perfect for gymnasts and people with good balance. One or more riders perform a series of tricky movements – bareback – on a horse that's being lunged.

Polocrosse

Popular in Australia, this fast game is a mixture of polo and lacrosse on horseback.

Be a sport!

Q I'd love to have a go at some of these sports, but don't know how to get involved. Who should I contact?

A First, have a chat with your instructor. You'd be surprised how many riding schools offer tuition in unusual sports such as side-saddle riding or even horseball. Another good bet is to contact national riding associations (you'll find some addresses on page 124). They can give you the address of a particular sport's governing body. Write to this and you should be able to find someone who teaches the sport in your area. You could join a riding or pony club. Many of these have teams that compete at showjumping, polo, one-day events and dressage.

13

What now?

BUYING A PONY • EQUESTRIAN CAREERS

If you enjoy riding and are passionate about ponies, the chances are you'll soon want more than a one-hour riding lesson, once a week. Maybe you're desperate for a pony of your own or are even thinking about a career with horses. The first step is to check out your options.

'I want a pony!'

You know what you want, your friends know what you want, but can you persuade your parents to let you have one? Ponies cost a lot of money and a great deal of time and commitment, so think carefully. Try looking after a pony for a week or two to see if you like it. Lots of riding schools organise holidays when you 'own' a pony for a while. If you do decide to buy, talk to your riding instructor and horsey friends, because they may know of a suitable pony. Otherwise, look through adverts in equestrian magazines or place your own 'wanted' advert, describing your ideal pony. Take an experienced person along with you when you look at a potential purchase and always get a pony examined by a vet before you hand over any cash.

Loaning 'n' sharing

A good alternative to buying a pony is to have one on loan or share one with a friend. Both arrangements can work well, provided you agree exactly who pays for what and put it in writing. Generally, if you have a pony on loan you are totally responsible for its daily care and exercise plus costs such as shoes, feed, livery (stabling) and vets' bills. Don't forget insurance, too. Sharing a pony allows you and a friend to split the costs, daily chores and riding between you. Again, make sure you know who's doing what when – your pony won't be happy if no-one gives it its tea, and you won't be happy if you turn up to find the pony gone!

'I want to work with horses!'

There are plenty of jobs in the horse industry, although many involve long hours, a lot of mucking-out and low pay. On the plus side, you'll get to meet loads of interesting people, enjoy plenty of riding and maybe even travel the world! Perhaps one of these careers is for you.

Farrier

This is the person who shoes your pony and cares for its feet. Farriers are usually male, simply because of the physical demands of the job – horses feet can be very heavy and many farriers retire early due to back strain!

Riding instructor

Just think – you could be teaching the future stars of the horse world! But remember, you'll have to give lessons in all weathers and do yard duties, too.

Saddler

Most of your time will be spent making or repairing pieces of tack so you'll have to have an eye for detail. You may also travel to riding schools or private yards to measure and fit ponies with saddles and bridles.

Groom

If you want to work for a famous showjumper, dressage rider or racehorse trainer, this is the job for you. Being a good groom often means doing 20 things at once – perfectly. You'll have to ride, muck out, plait, groom and travel with horses to events.

Equestrian journalist

You will be employed by a magazine or newspaper to write about horses. Most people start out as general journalists and specialise later on.

Take your pick...

If none of those jobs appeal, there are plenty of others to choose from. Gather together plenty of info about them all before you make a final decision.

- Vet
- Mounted police officer
- Veterinary nurse
- Veterinary sales rep
- Physiotherapist
- Jockey
- Vet
- Equine dentist
- Nutritionist
- Equine lecturer
- Chiropracter

Who to talk to:

Careers Advisors

When it is time for you to make a decision about your future career, ask your school's careers advisor for advice. He or she will be able to give you info about jobs in the horse industry, the qualifications you'll need and any training or courses that are available.

Join the club!

Whether you own a pony or are pony-mad but pony-less, joining a horsey club is a great way to meet other riders and improve your equine know-how. The Pony Club has lots of branches and offers tuition in riding and pony care plus the chance to compete in team sports ranging from polo to mounted games. Most branches also run fun 'pony camps' and shows. You'll find their address on page 124.

How did you score?

page 41 BRAINBUSTERS!

1. Stripe.
2. Throatlash.
3. Shetland.
4. In pain or angry.
5. Eggbut snaffle.
6. Arab.
7. Just above a pony's foot.
8. Yellow – the others are both types of roan.
9. An outside riding arena or school.
10. Dappled.

pages 100 & 101 PONY PUZZLERS

1. The nearside
2. 38° C.
3. Four.
4. They are types of curry comb.
5. Schoolmaster.
6. An upright has poles on one set of wings; a spread has two sets of wings.
7. False. A sepentine is a movement ridden in the school.
8. Choose from: whip, spurs, martingale.
9. Hay – this is a type of food, the others are all types of bedding for a pony's stable.
10. Sit.
11. Quick-release.
12. Choose from: leg-up, mounting block, vaulting.
13. In the school. They are referred to in the sentence to help you remember the letters around the school.

14. A dandy brush. It's used to remove mud from a pony's body.
15. The shape a pony makes when it rounds its back over a jump.
16. It refers to the right side of a pony.
17. By measuring them from your armpit to your fingertips.
18. The left foreleg.
19. Between the third and little finger and then between the first finger and thumb.
20. By sitting for two beats instead of one.

Want to know more?

USEFUL ADDRESSES • WEBSITES • BOOKS

Places to write to for more information...

**The British Horse Society,
British Equestrian Centre,**
Stoneleigh Park,
Kenilworth,
Warwickshire CV8 2LR.
• You can also contact the
Pony Club (GB) at this
address.

**Association of British Riding
Schools,**
Queens Chambers,
38–40 Queen Street,
Penzance,
Cornwall TR18 4BH.

**The Equestrian Federation of
Australia,**
52, Kensington Road,
Rose Park, SA 5067,
Australia.

**The New Zealand Equestrian
Federation,**
PO Box 47, Hastings,
New Zealand.

**South African National
Equestrian Federation,**
PO Box 374,
1748 Lanseria,
South Africa.

The Pony Club (Australia)
PO Box 46,
Lockhart,
New South Wales 2656,
Australia.

**Pony Club Association of NSW
Ltd**
RAS Showgrounds,
Moore Park,
Paddington,
NSW 2021,
Australia.

**The Horse Riding Centres
Association of Australia**
RMB 1275 Cooks Road,
Peats Ridge,
NSW 2250,
Australia.

The Pony Club (New Zealand)
Mr Scarlett,
10 Higginson Street,
PO Box 52,
Hawkes Bay,
New Zealand.

The Pony Club (South Africa)
Mrs Divov,
PO Box 32418,
Braamfontein 2017,
South Africa.

Surf the equine net

There are thousands of websites especially for pony-mad people, covering everything from model horses to breeds. For some horsey fun, try:

- Horsefun at http://horsefun.com/
- HorseWild!! at http://www.geocities.com/EnchantedForest/7731/
- The International Museum of the Horse at: http://www.imh.org
- Breeds info at http://www.equiworld.net/breeds/breedadd.htm
- Model horses at http://www.astroarch.com/modelhorse/
- Haynet at http://www.freerein.com/haynet/
- Horsenet at http://www.horsenet.com/
- Equinet at http://equinet.com/

Read all about it!

Pay a visit to your local library or bookshop and you'll find plenty of horsey reading. These are a few books that are well worth a look:

- Threshold Picture Guides, published by The Kenilworth Press.
- *The Manual of Horsemanship* (the official Pony Club Manual).
- *The Handbook of Riding* by Mary Gordon-Watson published by Pelham Books.
- *Rider's Guide to Mounted Games* by Toni Webber, published by Swan Hill Press.
- *A Young Person's Guide to Dressage* by Jane Kidd, published by Compass Equestrian.
- *Jumping Problems Solved* by Carol Mailer, published by Ward Lock.
- *Horse & Pony Care* by Jackie Budd, published by Ringpress Books.

Glossary

Don't understand a horsey term?
Check it out here

Aids The signals used by a rider to instruct their pony.

Bend The arc-shape of a pony's body as it turns.

Contact The link through the reins between a rider's hands and a pony's mouth.

Extended When a pony lengthens its stride so it covers more ground than normal.

Forward seat The position a rider adopts when jumping to stay in balance with their pony.

Grid A series of small jumps.

Impulsion The energy created by a pony's hindquarters.

Leading leg The pony's foreleg that stretches forward on its own when the pony is cantering.

Manege An enclosed riding arena.

Nearside The side from which you mount a pony – its left side.

Offside A pony's right side.

Placing pole A pole that is positioned in front of a jump to help a pony take off in the correct place.

Resistance Any attempt by a pony to disobey its rider's aids.

Seat The rider's position in the saddle.

Square halt When a pony stands still, with its weight evenly distributed on all four feet.

Transition The change from one gait to another.

Index

Index